LANTERNS, LAKES, & LARCENY

A Camper And Criminals Cozy Mystery

Book Twenty One

BY
TONYA KAPPES

D0896418

TONYA KAPPES
WEEKLY NEWSLETTER

Want a behind-the-scenes journey of me as a writer?
The ups and downs, new deals, book sales, giveaways and more? I share it all! Join the exclusive Southern Sleuths private group today! Go to www.patreon.com/Tonyakappesbooks

As a special thank you for joining, you'll get an exclusive copy of my cross-over short story, *A CHARMING BLEND.* Go to Tonyakappes.com and click on subscribe at the top of the home page.

The window shades were pulled closed, and when I went to knock on the door, I noticed the door was cracked.

"Hank! Jerry!" I called out to get them to join me.

"What?" Jerry made it around the corner first, and close by was Hank.

"The door is cracked, and I think what you heard was the television." I took a step back, knowing I wasn't armed like the two of them. If they wanted to open the door and find this Angus guy on the other end of a gun and not the receiving end, I didn't want to be the one to get shot.

"Angus? I'm Jerry." Jerry pushed open the door. "Aww, man." Jerry's voice turned raspy. He leaned on the doorjamb and gave a head tilt, indicating for Hank to look.

"What?" I asked when I noticed Hank's eye bulge and his inability to blink.

"Someone got to him before we did." Hank shoved the door open fully, letting the last bit of the day's sunlight filter in on Agnus Coo's body.

A pool of blood was around his head.

CHAPTER ONE

I'd never truly understood what it meant when Mary Elizabeth said, when I got my license many moons ago, that I drove like a bat out of hell, until today.

After a very long day where I'd not only found myself at the hands of a killer, but I'd also met the birth mother of my foster-adoptive brother, Bobby Ray Bonds, Hank Sharp, my ex-boyfriend and ex-sheriff, had called to tell me he was back in town.

Did I mention he followed that up with an "I miss you"? So yeah. I drove to Happy Trails Campground to meet up with him, like a bat out of hell.

"Hank?" I called through the dusty screen door of a fifth-wheel camper that was different than his last one.

He turned around, a little scruffier than the last time I'd seen him. He had a smile on his face underneath the beard and mustache, a couple of things he didn't have the last time I'd seen him.

"I hope you don't mind; I took my camper lot back." His beautiful green eyes danced. Those he did have the last time I'd seen him. "Can I ask you to come in?"

"Sure." I was hesitant. Not sure how to feel. "New camper?"

"Nah. I just got a good deal on it and traded up." His southern drawl was deep and made the words drawn out.

On the phone when he said he missed me, did he mean, like, *miss me* or just miss me? You knew the difference.

"I just put on some coffee." He pushed the little screen door handle down, and the door popped open. Chester, his dog, popped out. "Chester!"

He bounded out of the camper before I could even go inside. I bent down, and he jumped on me so hard that I fell on my heinie, which he took as an opportunity to give me a lot of kisses.

"I guess he missed you too." Hank, too, had stepped outside.

"I missed you guys." I played it up as no big deal.

"Huh, good to know." Hank put up his finger. "Let me get us a coffee, and do you think Chester could see Fifi?"

"I'm sure we can arrange it." I didn't tell him how when we'd gone hiking a few months ago, we'd found his lot down in Soggy Bottom. Fifi went crazy sniffing for Chester after she'd picked up the scent he'd left behind. I also left out the fact that we'd watched him drive off until the taillights were no longer visible.

"Here you go." His fingers grazed mine.

My heart ticked faster, and I sucked in a couple of quick breaths.

"You okay?" he asked. His deep voice and southern accent curled my toes.

"I'm good." Instead of telling him how I'd once again got myself into a very dangerous situation just a few hours ago, I just went with how I felt in this moment.

Actually, I was great. Fantastic, really. Even if we were broken up, I'd much rather him live here in my campground in the heart of the Daniel Boone National Forest instead of way across the state as a ranger at Mammoth Cave.

"You?" Carefully I sipped the hot coffee as we walked toward my little campervan I called home.

"Obviously, since I'm back, I had a few things I needed to work out." He kept his eyes forward and drank his coffee. "I didn't like the new position. Jerry Truman continued to call me about one of his cases and kept begging me to join him, so after saving a few people from cave spelunking, I took Jerry up on his offer."

I bit my tongue so I didn't say anything, though I wanted to scream for joy at the top of my lungs.

"That's where we need your help." First the beard—now his asking me for help really did knock me out of my socks.

"Yeah. Of course." I wanted to gloat and say, *Well, you mean to tell me that after years of you begging me to stop snooping around, meddlin' in other people's business, you now need my help?* "What's up?"

We stopped in front of my campervan. Fifi was already yipping inside. No doubt she could smell Chester.

Chester howled back.

Hank and I both laughed. Though he looked like a Grizzly Adams, his black hair, white teeth and gorgeous eyes told me he was right here.

"Fifi!" Hank bent down to pat her.

She slipped past him, and immediately Fifi and Chester darted off, running down the campground road and making their way around the lake until Chester chased her to the other side. Fifi jumped in the lake, knowing Chester would never follow her in. She was right.

Chester stood at the edge of the water, howling his little lungs out, tail wagging.

"Just like a woman. Poor Chester." Hank made a joke, but I wondered if it was really aimed at me.

"When are you going to shave that thing off?" I asked and reached over to give it a little tug.

"I was told women like a good beard." He winked. "I'd love to try it out on you." He leaned in a little.

"You would?" I questioned and leaned closer, and our lips touched. My heart sped up. My body tingled, even my hair.

"Maybelline Grant West!" Dottie Swaggert, Happy Trails Campground manager, squealed. "What is he doing here? You git! Git out of here!" Smoke rolled out of her mouth and trailed behind her cigarette as she waved her hands in the air.

CHAPTER TWO

"I heard you were here. I heard it straight, and sure enough, here you are." Dottie planted her hand on her hip and tapped the toe of her shoe. "You have some 'splaining to do if you think you're gonna drive that thing up in here and park. Or you're gonna have to start paying a lot fee."

"Good to see you, too, Dottie." Hank had a little sass to him, and that's why I'd fallen head over heels in love with him. We were a match made in campground heaven.

Literally.

I tended to be a little bit of a spitfire when I'd moved to Normal, Kentucky, our small tourist town, and when we first met, he didn't take anything off of me. He kept me accountable, more than any other man I'd ever had in my life—or person for that matter—and he loved me hard.

Maybe a little too hard, because he loved me so much, we broke up. That sounded pretty ridiculous, but I'd had a young boy in our town come and do some work around the campground. Things like pulling weeds, mucking the lake when it needed it, picking up trash around the campground, or even on the hiking trails. Just various little things.

I'd never imagined myself a mother, but after I taught him a few things, being a mother started to grow on me. I wasn't committing to anything, but I didn't rule it out either.

At the time, Hank was the sheriff of Normal, and he'd been working on a murder case. His hours were long, and his job was emotional. Hank didn't have a normal family life. Even though he had a mother and father, they didn't treat him well.

Neither of us had a traditional upbringing. I had wonderful parents, but unfortunately they were killed in our family house fire, leaving me an orphan, which was full circle as to why I had a foster-adoptive brother.

Anyways, I was on the fence about children, and Hank was completely off the fence. He claimed he could never do his job and be a present parent, so he left me. He loved me so much that he never wanted me to feel like I missed out on children and resent him for it years later.

It certainly wasn't years later. We were a couple of months later, and here he stood, right in front of my campervan.

"What do you have to say for yourself? I'd be 'shamed of you treatin' our May-bell-ine like you did. Left her standin' there all forlorn, tore up from the floor up." Dottie sucked in a draw of her cigarette before she pointed it directly at him. "You think you comin' in here lookin' like Paul Bunyan and all gonna steal May-bell-ine's heart again, you ain't. I'm here to tell you that if she can't."

"Dottie," I scolded her.

"It's okay, Mae." Hank stopped me. "Dottie is right. I didn't go about things right, and I regret it. But I'll prove to you that I'm on the up-and-up."

"What's that supposed to mean?" Dottie eyeballed him, and her chin slowly lifted in the air.

"I want to court Mae properly. Take her on dates. Put the past behind us and possibly work together." He didn't look at Dottie as he talked. He looked at me.

There was a calmness about him that I'd never seen before. Something was different, but I couldn't put my finger on it. Something very appealing. And I had missed his accent.

"Go on. I'm all ears." She wasn't going to let him off the hook that easily with his smooth talk, but I sure was.

"You'll see. Actions speak louder than words." He used one of Dottie's own sayings on her.

"You got that right." She threw the cig on the ground and snuffed it out with the toe of her shoe. She reached down to pick up the butt.

"Jerry rented the backroom from Gertrude Hobson for his new PI office. Do you think you could meet me there in the morning?" Hank asked me. "We will tell you about the case then."

Dottie was sticking to me like glue. She wasn't about to let any words be spoken that she couldn't hear.

"I'll be there around nine a.m." I was happy it was Dottie's turn to work the morning shift at the campground office. Though all the guests had checked in for the week, we still had someone in the office for anything they might need.

"Perfect." He ran his hand down my arm and clasped my hand. "I wasn't lying when I told you I missed you."

"I missed you too." It was like we were magnets. We leaned in, and Dottie shoved her hand between our faces.

"Nope. Uh-un. Nah. Ain't gonna happen 'til I see you doin' what you 'sposed to be doin'." She didn't dare budge.

"I'll see you tomorrow." Hank smiled. He whistled, and Chester came running, Fifi still swimming around. She'd forgotten about Chester. She was with the ducks.

Hank walked off and into his camper.

"Dottie, what was that about?" The frustration fell upon me harder and harder with each step Hank had taken away from me. "You're not my mother."

"I certainly am not, you're right. I'm your friend. Friends keep friends sane when hunky ex-boyfriends come around." She threw a chin down his way. "That boy's got more moves than a Slinky going down an escalator."

"I like Slinkys." I snickered and took the biggest and deepest breath I'd taken in a really long time.

CHAPTER THREE

F ifi and I slept better that night than we had in weeks.

"Good morning." I rolled over and pulled the curtain away from the camper bedroom window to look down toward Hank's lot. "It was real," I said with a sigh and rolled back over on my back.

I looked up at the ceiling and couldn't stop myself from smiling. Many times since Hank was gone, I found myself looking down at the empty lot that I'd yet to let anyone rent. It was a prime lot too.

Happy Trails Campground was a campground for the Daniel Boone National Park. I had every type of camp. Lots with all the hookups for campers—all classes, bungalows of varying sizes, and a spot for tent campers.

There was a big lake in the middle with a road going around it. There were several roads that went off the main road that led to different parts of the campground, but most people loved to be around the lake and near the office and recreational facility.

There were several trailheads along the tree line of the campground and off of Red Fox Trail, and I offered fishing, kayaking, canoeing, swimming, and white-water rafting activities for an extra fee. Alvin Deters, a local store owner and ex-kayak champion, and I had gone into business down by the water, where he offered lessons to my guests.

It'd become a real big business over the last three years, and I was very grateful for living here.

But it was the seasons that took my breath away.

There was never a prettier time in Kentucky or the Daniel Boone Forest than the fall. This morning in particular, everything was almost too pretty to look at.

It could've possibly been my state of mind, or euphoria, but I believed the bright sun dripping down the mountainous backdrop was giving the red, orange, yellow, and green leaves on the trees a spotlight in which to shine.

It was like a switch had been flipped from yesterday's heat wave to today's fall-like weather. That was how it was in Kentucky. One day it was sweltering, and the next it was snowing. It was fine with me. I loved all seasons, and Kentucky had all four.

I swung my legs off the side of the bed and slipped on my sweat-shirt. I pulled the hair tie off my wrist and put my curly hair up in a bun to get it off my shoulders. Fifi jumped off the bed and ran to the door for her morning potty break.

On my way past the kitchenette, I flipped on the coffee pot and didn't bother getting Fifi's leash from the basket next to the door since it was morning and any creatures that would want to eat her as a snack had gone back into the forest to hide until they were hidden under the dark of the night.

"Let's go potty." I unlocked the campervan door and opened it, only to find Betts Hager, Abby Fawn-Bonds, Queenie French, and Dottie all sitting at my picnic table underneath the camper awning. "Glad to see you brought donuts."

There was a box from the local bakery, The Cookie Crumble, along with a box of coffee from there as well.

"Did I miss a meeting?" I asked my group of friends, called the Laundry Club Ladies since we mainly liked to hang out at the Laundry Club Laundromat, owned by Betts. "I thought the book club was tomorrow night." I tapped my temple. "Or did Abby or Dottie tell y'all about Hank?" My tone went up an octave in delight.

"Yes!" Betts clapped her hands in happiness. "And we want to hear all about it."

"I told you 'bout it." Dottie nudged her and took a bite of a chocolate glazed donut with fall-colored sprinkles.

"I want to hear about it from Mae's point of view. Is he still just as dreamy as you thought he was?" Betts asked as if Hank had been gone for years.

"He does have a beard and mustache, but still so sweet, and those eyes." I groaned as my teeth sank down into a strawberry-and-cream-filled long john.

"I love a good, burly, mustached man." Queenie rolled her head around on her neck, not touching the donuts in fear she'd mess up her sixty-something-year-old figure. After all, she had to keep up the persona she had as the local Jazzercise franchise owner and instructor.

"I can't wait to see him." Abby, my new sister-in-law, beamed. "I wish y'all could've seen her face yesterday afternoon at the median when she got his phone call."

"Y'all forget just yesterday I helped Tucker and Al catch a killer. None of you have asked about it." Though I tried to stay present in the conversation, my mind was ticking the time away until I met Hank at Trails Coffee Shop at nine this morning.

"You are fine. I heard Violet's report on the news last night, and she didn't even mention you. Al Hemmer was all over it." Betts shook her head. "We came here to hear all about Hank and the kiss."

"Dottie." My jaw dropped, and I looked at her.

"Did you think I was going to not tell them?" She didn't hide the fact she had loose lips.

Fifi ran back over and waited next to Dottie. She knew where she was going to get some food. And Dottie delivered.

"Dottie," I scolded her again.

"I gave her a pinch. A pinch of donut isn't going to kill that dog." She picked up her cigarette case, snapped it open at the top, and batted out a cigarette. She stuck it in the corner of her mouth, where it could stay for minutes to up to an hour unlit. "Don't be takin' the heat off of you and puttin' it on me." She swung her finger around to point at everyone else. "Go on, y'all give her a piece of your mind." Dottie's face was as red as her hair, she was so beside herself about Hank Sharp being back in town and at the campground.

"I'm so excited to see what's next." Abby was a romantic at heart. She had to be to have fallen head over heels in love with Bobby Ray, the least romantic person I knew. "Do you think he'll go back to the sheriff's department?"

"No. He's actually working for Jerry Truman's private investigation business. Gert Hobson is letting them rent that little room she uses for storage in the back of her coffee shop, so that's where I'm meeting them this morning. He said he needed my help, but I'm not sure with what." I put the paper cup under the spout of the box coffee container and got me a cup, even though the aroma of the fresh pot of coffee I'd made in the camper floated out of the screen door.

"Interesting." Queenie lifted her arms and did arm rolls out to the side a few times before she shifted them up in the air. "I hope you told him the Laundry Club Ladies are still just as good as before he left."

"I'm sure we will all be doing some sort of snooping around." I wiggled my brows. "About that kiss," I reminded them because I couldn't wait to tell them about the itchy beard and the almost-kiss before Dottie had stopped it with her hand.

I left the ladies gushing and headed back inside after I took another donut to get ready for my date—um, business meeting with Hank.

CHAPTER FOUR

My mood was so good that my fuzzy hair didn't bother me a bit. Normally I'd be trying to tame the curls, but instead, I let them spring up all over and any way they wanted.

I slipped into a pair of jeans, a short-sleeved V-neck white top, and a pair of strappy, low-heeled sandals. I hardly wore makeup anymore, but I did swipe some red lipstick across my lips and put on a little bit of mascara.

Fifi sat outside of the bathroom, watching me.

"Don't you be giving me any grief." I shook the mascara wand at her before I put away the little bit of makeup I did keep in the camper.

Space was limited, so anything I brought in had to be a must or carefully planned out to where it would go. When I'd gotten to Normal and realized this was actually going to be my home, I had stripped the campervan down to the bare nubbins.

I'd redone the entire thing with the blessings of YouTube videos, some freebies, a loan from Alvin Deters, and the goodwill of people who didn't know me.

It had really become home. I never thought I'd live in the tiny house on wheels, but I loved it.

Cozy was how I would describe it, and at night when it was dark, I'd consider it romantic with all the twinkly lights I'd strung.

I'd bought a used Ford Focus from Grassle's Garage, the only gas station and local car garage downtown. Joel Grassle was a good guy and even gave Bobby Ray a job when he'd come to town. Only Joel had had no idea just how talented Bobby Ray was, and even Joel had learned a few things from him.

"You be a good girl." I made sure Fifi had fresh water and was settled before I headed out. "I'll be back in a few hours. Dottie will let you out." I grabbed the Focus keys and locked the camper door behind me.

I turned the radio on, hummed along to the latest pop song, and beat my finger on the wheel, taking each curve with ease. The roads in the forest were small one-lane roads with hairpin curves. Even an inch off the shoulder were fifty-foot drop-offs, and staying alert was a must.

The trees lining the road made a beautiful canopy with dots of sunshine filtering through. A gorgeous day was on tap, and having Hank in my life again did make everything seem a little bit happier. Though I wasn't sure where we stood, all I knew was that it felt better having him in it than out of it.

Trails Coffee was located on the right side of downtown Normal. The roads were one-way and divided by a grassy median, where there were picnic tables and an amphitheater among the large oak trees. The grassy median was always packed, and this morning was no different.

Just like the cottage-style shops located downtown, they all had a side yard, and Gert had put out café tables along with a coffee stand for her customers.

I pulled into a spot along the road and parked.

"Good morning, Mae. Hank told me you'd be here." Gert Hobson saw me come in the door of Trails Coffee. "Are you just thrilled he's back in town?"

"I wish I wasn't so happy, but I am." The smile just wouldn't stop growing.

"Are you two back together?" she whispered and let her employees take over the counter while we chatted for a minute.

"I don't know. I do know that he kissed me." It was a start, and even though I was thirty years old and acting this way, I didn't care. He made me happy, and I was going to try to figure out a way for us to work out. "I slept the best I've slept in a couple months last night."

"That's saying something." She gave me a hug. "I'm happy for you. There'll be a wedding in no time. Mary Elizabeth will surely have a duck fit planning a daughter's wedding."

"Gives me a headache thinking about it," I joked, knowing what she said was exactly right.

Mary Elizabeth had been talking about me getting married for years, and then when I snuck off to New York City as soon as I turned eighteen, I stole that dream from her. But the nail in the coffin was when I'd gotten married to a man much older than me and she had to read about it in the paper. That had probably hurt her the most.

I'd spent the better part of the past year making it up to her. I can only imagine what she was going to think about Hank coming back.

"You better get back there. Hank and Jerry are already having some of the Harvest Blend coffee without you." She plucked a cup from the counter with someone else's name written on it. "You can have this one, and I'll make another one."

"Thank you." I took a quick sip. Gert had her own nationwide coffee company and was a master roaster. Her seasonal roasts were so good, and I looked forward to the fall and winter roasts. "Delish." I wagged it up in the air on my way back to the storage-room-turned-private-investigator-office.

The door was slightly ajar. I peeked in with one eye to assess what I was about to walk into because I wasn't good in blind situations.

Jerry and Hank were bent over a small desk, looking at something. They were pointing and murmuring. They had a few cups of coffee that appeared to be empty lying on the floor, and they each had one in their hands. From what it appeared, they'd been there awhile.

"Nine o'clock on the dot." I opened the door.

"Mae." Hank sighed and came over.

"Your beard? I just can't get used to it." I couldn't help but blush looking at his unshaven face. The man I loved was still there, and his smile guided me to smile back. "You are so handsome."

"You're beautiful." He put his hand around my waist, pulled me to him, and kissed me.

"Honestly, this is a real office. A place of business. Not make-out hill." Jerry Truman groaned.

"Hi, Jerry." I was fond of Jerry and his wife, Emmalyn. "You look like you've lost some weight."

"Thank you for noticing." Jerry was six feet tall, and he did have a belly that hung over his pants, but it wasn't hanging today. "Ever since I left the sheriff's office and stopped eating donuts all day, I've gotten a little healthier."

"Don't let him fool you," Hank teased. "Emmalyn has him on a strict diet."

"Good for you. You look great." I walked over to see what they'd been looking at. "I guess I'm at a loss for what I'm doing here."

There were a few notes on the desk. A couple of handwritten ones, along with a few that looked like cut-out letters from magazines and newspapers.

"Jerry called me a week or so ago, and as usual keeps asking me to join his private investigating team."

"The old boy finally took me up on my offer. I knew if I bugged him enough, he'd join." Jerry smacked Hank on the back, the good-ole-boy way. "I could tell he wasn't happy back in the ranger field and away from you." Jerry pointed at me.

"True on both." Hank laid a hand on the small of my back.

"Good to see you two back together." Jerry nodded.

"Are we?" I looked at Hank.

"You've let me kiss you twice now." Hank gave me an odd look.

"I thought that was a friend kiss." I winked. "We have a lot to talk about between us when Jerry isn't around."

The conversation was awkward in front of Jerry, but we did need to discuss things. Hank made me extremely happy, but we still hadn't talked about what broke us up in the first place.

"Is that why I'm here?" I needed to change the subject.

"Heck no. I don't care if you ever get back with him. What I care about is this case I've got. I told Hank if anyone can help us figure this one out, it'd be you." Jerry picked up a letter. "We have a woman who is getting all sorts of death threats by letters. Nothing has happened yet, but it's been enough to make her scared. She has hired us to find out who is sending them."

"How can I help with that?" I asked.

"Judie Doughty is our client." Jerry picked up a file off the desk, opened it, and took out a photo. "She is big into fundraising for Hopes with Horses. She started it years ago, but now that it's taken off, it's become a nonprofit and very successful."

"Yeah. Is that the foundation where they use horses for all sorts of therapy?" I'd seen articles in the paper about it.

"It is." Jerry handed me a brochure for the upcoming fundraiser.

"Yes. I heard about this. Coke mentioned how busy they were going to be and called Happy Trails to see if we could accommodate some of the out-of-town guests." I frowned. "Unfortunately, we are booked up into next summer."

It was crazy just how popular camping, campers, and anything outdoors had become over the past few years. We rarely had a cancellation, but when we did, the spot was immediately booked by the next person in line.

"The fundraiser is tonight, and we all need to be there." Jerry sure didn't give me a lot of time to prepare for going. "But I want to give you a list of places Judie goes frequently so you can snoop around."

"What kind of places?" I wondered why they wanted me to do this.

"The hairdresser, for one. It would be silly if we went in to see Helen Pyle with all sorts of questions. Both of us ex-sheriffs snooping around into a client's life when Judie doesn't want anyone to know about the letters." Jerry made a good point.

Jerry's phone rang, and he excused himself from the room, leaving Hank to tell me the rest.

"Judie hasn't told anyone about the letters, but she's feeling like something might happen at the fundraiser because one of the letters has a photo of fireworks on it. Judie said she's having a huge fireworks display right before they announce the amount donated for the evening." Hank handed me a piece of paper with various places Judie had gone. "We've pretty much taken care of the ones that are crossed out, but the Cute-icles has your name written all over it."

"This is a far cry from how you acted before you left for the Mammoth Cave post." I couldn't keep myself from reminding him of how he had hated when I put my nose into these types of situations before.

"Listen, we've not had time to talk about me coming home. But I realized after I got to the new post and had time to get away from Normal and all the stress from going from ranger to detective—then throw in the sheriff position when Jerry left—that I was wrong."

"Wrong?" I teased, letting him know I really liked hearing that word come out of his mouth.

"I was wrong." He stared at me. Very serious. "I wanted so badly to protect you that I ended up smothering you. No wonder you didn't ever listen to me plead with you not to put yourself in danger. I should have known better. I knew you'd never do anything to get hurt, but as the sheriff and your boyfriend, I couldn't let anything happen to you. The thought of if it did crushed me. I'd never be able to live with myself."

"Now? What's different?" I needed to know before there was a thing between us.

"I want to work with you. I don't want to be against you. As the sheriff, I had the law to uphold, and now I just have you to hold. At least that's what I'm hoping." He ran his hand through his dark hair. "Mae, I love you so much it hurts. I've never loved a woman that hard. You are so smart, kind, and just a good person. That's who I want by my side for my life. I know you love fierce and loyal. No matter what we do, I know that we need to do it together. So I took Jerry up on his job, and when I talk about work, I can feel free to talk about it with you. I can feel good asking you to go into the salon and ask questions because I know you will use your mind. And with me in this position, I don't need you to hide from me who you are and keep things from me like when you did when I was sheriff."

In a roundabout way, in Hank's way, he was telling me that he loved me and accepted me for me.

"We are a team." He dragged his finger between us. "Me and you in everything we do. Work, play, love, and family. Forever."

This wasn't a marriage proposal, but it was pretty good.

"What do you say we take another stab at us?" He took a couple of steps over to me. "Me and you. That's all that matters."

"Kids?" I questioned the sore subject.

"As long as they look like you." He smiled, pulling me to him, and gave me a kiss.

"Seriously? Can you two please concentrate on our client?" Jerry walked back into the room.

"We are back together." Hank held me tight. "I feel so much better."

"Great. So that was Judie. She said that everything is all set for the fundraiser and she's got the entire guest list waiting for us at the entrance of the barn."

"At the Old Train Station Motel, right?" I needed all the details.

"Right." Jerry handed me a piece of paper. "That's Judie's phone number. I also gave her yours just in case she needs one of us."

"What are your initial thoughts?" Hank sincerely asked me how I felt about a case for the first time.

"I am going to go to see Helen at Cute-icles, and I think I'll stop by and talk to Coke to see if anyone had come around asking about the fundraiser or Judie." It seemed like a logical place to start. "Before we do that, why does she think someone would want to kill her?"

"She doesn't know, but that would be a good place for you to question her. Woman to woman?" Jerry asked.

"We have a series of questions we've come up with to ask clients when they want to hire us. In this case we asked about her husband, children, and anyone on the Hopes with Horses committee, but she said that she couldn't think of anyone." Hank had flipped through a notebook like the one he used to use when he was a detective.

It was cute seeing that little notebook again, but this time it was much better being on this side of him and not the side where he rolled his eyes at me.

"Obviously we are trying to get to the bottom of this before anyone gets killed." Jerry's point was the most important.

"I think I need to talk to her then." I thought it would be a good idea to get my intuitive instinct on Judie. "I'll keep in touch."

"Sounds good. We will all meet at the fundraiser around seven-ish?" Jerry looked between us.

"I can," Hank agreed.

"Me too." I put the phone number in my pocket and gave Hank a kiss goodbye. "I'll let you know if I find out anything." I took one of the notebooks off the desk since I didn't have my own.

"Stay safe," Hank said with a little bit of the old Hank coming out.

CHAPTER FIVE

I nstead of walking across the street to Cute-icles, where I would definitely question Helen Pyle first, I decided to go on out to Fawn Road, where the Old Train Station Motel was located. Cute-icles was closed, and I didn't feel like sitting around waiting for it to open.

Coke Ogden had really exceeded all expectations when she'd taken on the Old Train Station, which had been abandoned, and turned it into the Old Train Station Motel.

The actual structure was centuries old and was a real train station that had been a source of travel to and from the Daniel Boone National Park.

The massive concrete station was beautiful, framed by the dramatic backdrop of the mountains of the national park. There were a lot of trails around the area, and most of them were the more difficult trails to hike. However, I'd recently opened a new one that was less strenuous since I'd been appointed to the National Park Committee.

I loved sitting on the committee because it gave me the opportunity to help with growth and get to know a lot of people, which made my meddling around seem not so much like snooping.

I pulled my car up and parked in front of the middle of the motel. I loved looking at the domed, circular, open courtyard area with six massive concrete pillars holding up a dramatic patina metal roof with a rooster weather vane.

It was the most ornamental part of the motel and so pretty. The motel had a total of ten guest rooms, five on each side of the middle dome.

There was going to have to be a time when Coke added on, because she was getting just as booked as the campground, especially since she'd taken advantage of the old barns and outbuildings she'd turned into venues for things such as weddings, showers, birthday parties, and fundraisers.

Coke was standing in the middle of the dome when I got out to go look for her. It was unusual to see her with her shoulder-length blond hair pulled back into a ponytail, since I'd only seen her wear it down and flipped up at the ends.

"Mae, what on earth are you doing here?" she asked with delight. "Can I get you a sweet tea?"

I did love some good sweet tea, and Coke did make some mighty fine tea for her guests that she served at the Old Train Station's Caboose Diner.

"I'm good, but you are busy today, I hear." I wanted to be respectful of her time since she was standing over a large vase, arranging flowers.

"It's going to be a big one tonight." She took a step back, ogling the arrangement from all angles before she dug her hand back in it and moved the long stems around. "Plus the weather has turned out gorgeous for the event."

"Yeah. That's why I'm here." I knew Coke would know exactly what I was up to if I tried to beat around the bush, so I didn't. "Hank and I are sorta back together."

"Oh my God, you want to plan a wedding!" Coke threw her hands up to her mouth.

"No. No, no." I shook my head but couldn't stop the smile. Her excitement was contagious. "But I am happy, though a tad bit leery."

"I understand that. But what's going on?" she asked.

"Hank and Jerry are in the private investigator business now, and

Judie Doughty is their client. She's been getting some pretty nasty notes in the mail, and we are going to be here tonight to make sure things go smoothly," I told her.

"Should I get Al Hemmer?" Coke's brows knotted.

"Nothing like that. We have it covered, plus there's a guest list, so there shouldn't be any surprise guests. I'm here now just to see if you've noticed anyone slinking around. Snooping with questions?" I thought that would be a good place to start.

"Not that I can recall," Coke responded. "I've only dealt with Delaney Harrison, the horse trainer, Judie's husband, Powell, and her son Evan. They've all been easy to work with."

I jotted down the names Coke had rattled off and who they were to Judie just for reference.

"Do you know how tonight is going to go?" I asked.

"There's an itinerary she wants us to follow. There will be the auction of the main horses. I'm sure it'll be crazy, seeing how these are some really fine thoroughbreds. The guest list is very expensive."

"Expensive?" What did that mean?

"A lot of high-dollar people. Millionaires." She sighed. "All those millionaires in one place. That's crazy to me. But since Judie won the mega power lottery—the big one—I suspect she was welcomed with open arms."

"She won the mega power lottery?" I didn't recall Hank or Jerry mentioning that, which was a huge detail to leave out and a great motive for death threats.

"Oh dear. I thought you'd know since she hired you." Coke had a worried look on her face. "I guess I shouldn't've said anything. From what I gathered, not many people know she won because she was one of those who claimed the prize anonymously."

"I wouldn't be able to keep my big mouth shut. Would you?" I snorted.

"I'd be skipping all over town, yelling it out into the world." Coke made me laugh out loud. "If I hear anything, I'll keep you posted. Other than that, it's all I know or have seen. I'm sorry I couldn't be any help."

"You're more help than you realize." I thanked her and told her I'd see her later tonight.

After I got back in the car, I sat there for a few minutes to collect my thoughts so I could write down everything Coke had mentioned.

"The fact Judie won the mega power lottery gives me a good motive." I looked over the names of people Coke had mentioned. If they were in Judie's inner circle, they'd probably have some insight into just who might be sending the letters.

Delaney Harrison, Evan Doughty, and Powell Doughty were definitely on my list of people to see tonight at the fundraiser.

CHAPTER SIX

I nstead of calling Hank and Jerry to let them know what I'd found out about the lottery, I figured I'd just head back to downtown now that Cute-icles was open for business. If I found out anything from Helen, then I'd go back over to the office and let them know everything I'd found out.

There wasn't a parking space on the street, so I drove past Cute-icles and pulled into the Laundry Club parking lot at the far end of the street.

It wasn't like Cute-icles was far. It was just a few shops down, and walking in the fresh air was so good. It helped my brain get oxygen and clear the way for some good old-fashioned sleuthing.

Even when I wasn't on a mission to get some information or trying to get some clues, sitting in Helen's chair and just listening to the ladies gossip was well-informed entertainment.

The beauty parlor, like the rest of the shops in downtown Normal, was an old house. In front of the shop was an old-fashioned wooden sign with the shop's name and a spotlight positioned below it. The pale-yellow house had cute gingerbread latticework along the top, which made it very cozy and welcoming. It was the downtown area of Normal that added the extra touch to the Daniel Boone National Forest that made our cozy little town nestled in the mountains a wonderful place to vacation.

Since it was an old house, Helen didn't do much to change the rooms, so when you walked in there was a family room on the right and a dining room on the left. The hallway led you straight back to the familiar smell of hair products and the sound of chatter.

"Hey, Mae," Helen greeted me. She had her scissors in one hand and a comb in the other, clipping away on Pam Purcell's hair. The colorful gem-beaded shirt she'd bedazzled sparkled when the overhead lights hit it just right. "I didn't see you on the books today. Not that you're not there. I swear my eyes are getting worse by the day."

I leaned against the counter and looked around the salon with the Pepto Bismol-colored walls. I wanted to see who was in there and who might know about Judie's visit.

"Don't you be fiddling with my hair then." Pam Purcell leaned forward enough to be out of Helen's arm's reach.

"Not that kind of eyesight. I can see perfectly when doing hair." Helen didn't make much sense, but I went with it, and so did Pam.

Pam eased back, curled her nose, and rolled her eyes.

"Not much you can do to mess up my hair anyways," Pam grumbled as Helen began to cut away on Pam's already-short hair.

"If you'd let it grow instead of coming in here weekly," Carol Wise, one of Pam's best friends and worst enemies, said from across the room. She was lying in one of the reclined chairs with her head in the shampoo bowl, with Lib Tuttle, one of Helen's best friends, running the water sprayer through Carol's hair to get out the shampoo and whatever other chemicals Helen had put in Carol's hair.

"I'd talk." Pam's head didn't move, but her eyes shifted to the side to look at me. "Mae, I've got some great apple butter just in time for fall right over there. Take you a jar. I heard Hank was back at the campground, and he loves my apple butter."

"Tucker told me Hank quit the rangers." Helen snickered. "Good thing you got rid of him. That boy can't keep a job. One minute he's an agent with the FBI, which we could've used more around here with all the drugs being smuggled through the forest, but whatever floats his boat."

"That's when he wanted to be a ranger." Carol tsked. "Then that partner of his got killed, so I guess he tried his hand at sheriff. Which if I had the choice, I'd much rather have Hank than Al."

They spoke as if I wasn't even there.

"Mm-hmm." Pam decided to put her two cents in. "Now he's back and doing some sort of private investigating work or something. I don't know. I saw Agnes Swift at the church's spaghetti supper last week, and she told me he was coming home to do this new job."

"Ahem." I cleared my throat just to make sure they did remember I was there.

"I'm happy to say Hank and I are trying to work through some things." I wanted to make it abundantly clear, because if I didn't, their gossip would be switched, twisted, and knotted up with untruths when it got back to me or Hank about me being at the salon.

"We are so happy for you. Aren't we, girls?" Helen commanded the entire conversation.

"Yes. He's a doll." Pam smiled.

"He is. And he's so good to his granny," Carol mentioned as Lib sat her up, towel-drying Carol's hair.

"Lib, you working here now?" I asked Lib.

"Nah. I was over at the boutique, looking at all the fall clothes Carrie Patillo got in." She pointed to a pile of bags next to a puffy chair. "Go on and look. I stopped by to show them to Helen, and she's gabbing so much, she's backing up. Carol's pretty, long black hair might have fallen out if I didn't get her out of them foils." Lib snickered.

"Mae, what are you here for?" Helen asked.

I walked over to the fluffy chair to sit down while I looked at the clothes Lib had gotten from the boutique.

"I'm actually here because I'm helping Hank and Jerry on a case." I didn't bother glancing up to see their faces, because I could feel the wind created from them whipping their heads around. "This is so cute."

I held up one of the shirts Lib had gotten. "I need to go over and see Carrie and pick up some new clothes."

"So it's true? Hank decided to leave law enforcement altogether?" Lib asked. She and Carol walked over. Lib pulled more clothes out and let Carol get a closer look.

"It is. I haven't talked to him about living plans, but for now he's pulled his fifth-wheel back into the campground, like Helen heard, and is working with Jerry. They got an office in the back of Trails Coffee. Gert is letting them use the storage room, and it's pretty neat. They've got a few clients, and I'm here because one of their clients, Judie Doughty, was in here getting her hair done." I shifted my focus to Helen.

"She was in here this morning." Helen shook her comb before she went back to running it through Pam's hair. "She's been in here one other time, like five years ago. From what I heard, she's been pretty much a recluse. Then she came in here and didn't spare no expense. She got her a manicure from Sally Ann and a pedicure. She even got a brow wax, and boy, did she need it."

"Did you hear about that big fundraiser she's having for Hopes for Horses or something like that?" Carol started the gossip.

"Hopes for Horses? What do horses hope for?" Pam snarled.

"She's doing good things like therapy for people or something like that." Helen had no idea.

"No." Lib shook her head. "I think it has something to do with a national organization or something, and she's just hosting a fundraiser for it."

"Why on earth would she do something like that?" Helen sighed.

"Beats me." Pam opened the *Country Living* that was sitting in her lap and started to thumb through it.

"Where is Sally Ann?" I looked around. "When I came in, the front room was empty."

"She's gone over to get us a snack from the diner," she said. "She should be back any minute."

Sally Ann was the manicurist at the Cute-icles. She used the front family room part of the house to work on her clients' nails.

Just about that time, we all heard the front door open.

"Sally Ann? That you?" Helen yelled.

"Hold your horses!" Sally Ann hollered back. "I'm coming."

"Speaking of horses—" I laughed at the irony and waved to Sally Ann when she walked in with a sack full of food. "I heard Judie Doughty came in to see you this morning."

"You heard right." She put the sack on the counter and opened it to take out various-sized boxes. "I got us some biscuits for your apple butter," she told Pam.

"Keep one jar for Maybelline to take to Hank." Pam was hell-bent on me taking that apple butter.

"I heard you two were..." Sally Ann finished her sentence with a wink and click of her tongue.

"They sure are, and Hank's even opened himself up his own business." Helen got it half right, but enough for me not to correct her. "You got you a problem with someone, he can fix it."

"He's not a hit man. He's a private investigator, and Judie has been getting some threats against her life." I watched Sally Ann's face to see if she had any reaction.

"I reckon you would, too, if you won the big lottery." Sally Ann opened the lids of the boxes.

"Won the lottery?" The women all gasped.

"Oops." Sally Ann threw her hand over her mouth. "I don't think I was supposed to mention that, but now that it's out, she did."

If I was a betting woman, I would bet Sally Ann had been itching to let that slip from the time Judie told her.

"She said that people came out of the woodwork like carpenter ants. People she'd not heard of since childhood. People she didn't even know had left letters and requests in her mailbox." Sally Ann kept on telling everything she knew. "Can you imagine? Anyways, she said something about notes, but all I kept thinking about was how I was holding a millionaire's hand in mine and honestly we are no different."

"Nah. Just a little difference of a lot of millions compared to your bank account." Helen laughed.

"I'm saying she brushes her hair no different than we brush ours." Sally Ann made a strange analogy, but we all went with it.

"So she didn't mention anything about notes or who could possibly have written notes to her?" I asked. "I know how people start talking when they come in here."

Really, what was it about a salon or any sort of beauty treatment chair, even the chair of the manicurist, that made us talk and tell some of our deepest secrets?

"Not a word. She did invite me to the big fundraiser and gave me a pretty good tip. She probably hoped I was going to come there tonight and give it back for the fundraiser, but I ain't." She took a plastic knife out of one of the cabinet drawers and stuck it in the apple butter jar before she slopped a big glop of it on her biscuit. "She also talked about their lifestyle change. They were dirt poor before the money had come along, and they were able to barely get by, but now that they have the foundation and she can help people, it's changed all of their lives by giving them all jobs, and more importantly, a purpose in life. Especially her son. She said he didn't know what he wanted for his life. All she had to their name was a good breeding horse, and they scraped together enough money to hire one trainer. That's about it."

Helen Pyle walked over after she put Pam under a hair dryer.

"I know you're not here for any services, but it's time for your lowlights. I've got a couple of hours if you've got a couple of hours." She looked at the bun on top of my head. "From what I see, there's growth from the summer lights."

"Sure. Why not?" I pulled my hair out of the bun.

"This is really good apple butter." Lib slapped some more on another biscuit.

"Did you try my peach jam?" Carol blurted out.

"You can't stand it, Carol," Pam teased Carol. They'd had a long-standing feud on who had the best jams, pies, and anything else you could make with fruit, for as long as I'd known them.

Carol stalked over to the chair Pam was sitting in.

"I can too stand it." Carol shook a finger. "Just you wait and see. Next month at Chicken Fest, I'll beat your apple butter with my jam."

Pam stood up. She was about half a foot taller than Carol and half a foot wider. She wasn't a big woman, maybe five feet six, but her voice was louder than Carol's squeakier voice that held more southern sarcasm, which I could tell was getting under Pam's skin. Carol's long black strands were dripping wet.

"What are you looking at?" Carol put her hands on her thin hips and jutted them to the side.

"You're on." Pam put her hand out, and the two of them shook on it.

I liked Pam and Carol. They were just good folk that took pride in their businesses and a friendly game of competition.

CHAPTER SEVEN

The Chicken Fest was just one of many festivals that took place in Normal during the year. This particular festival took place during the fall, and it wasn't until next month. With Pam and Carol talking about it, it was all I could think of the rest of the day.

The entire state of Kentucky celebrated Chicken Fest, which was a homage to Colonel Sanders and his famous fried chicken he'd brought to our great state.

It was also the time when Ty Randal did his best to replicate the Colonel's secret recipe.

"Did you know Chicken Fest is coming up?" My mouth watered at the thought, even asking Hank the question.

"I haven't thought about it, but I guess it is." He looked over at me. His grin lifted to his eyes. They appeared much greener as they reflected off the black tuxedo he'd worn for the fundraiser. "Why on earth are you thinking about that?"

We stood in the back of one of the working horse barns, where the foals were all lined up to be walked outside in the horse ring for the bidding to begin. Jerry Truman was bringing the earpieces for us to wear so we could communicate during the fundraiser as we kept our eyes open for any unusual activity.

"When I was at Cute-icles today, Pam and Carol were there, which reminds me, I have some apple butter from Pam for you." By the time I'd gotten back to Happy Trails to work the afternoon shift in the office and be home in time to take Fifi for a quick walk, feed her, and get presentable for the fundraiser, I'd forgotten to take Hank his apple butter.

"We are going to the same place tonight. You can give it to me then." He lifted his chin when he noticed Jerry walking through the field. "Or better yet, we can have it over breakfast in the morning."

Hank sure was pulling out all the stops now that we were working on our relationship. It was a different side of him. He was more attentive to putting us first, which was a switch when he was working. I liked it.

"Sorry I'm late." Jerry huffed. "Emmalyn had to take up my pants since I've not had this monkey suit on since, well, I guess I got married."

"It looks great. Did she come tonight?" I asked in hopes I'd see her.

"Nah. This is a job. She stayed home, but she did say to tell you that she wants to grab some coffee and catch up." He moved on to the reason we were here. "Here are the earpieces. We can talk to each other like we are now, and it all should be clear. Hank and I will cover any and all things we see as a threat, while I'd like for you to do what you do best." He grinned. "Talk to people. People in Judie's circle to see if they know anything."

"You mean if they have a reason to blackmail her?" I assumed her family were on Jerry's list of people who could possibly want a little piece of the pie. "Judie hasn't been keeping her winnings a secret. She might not be putting it on the news," I corrected myself, "but she is certainly telling people she won. She told Sally Ann, who in turn ended up telling everyone in the beauty salon. When I asked Sally Ann about the notes, she mentioned Judie told her that she gets notes all the time in her mailbox."

"Did she say what the notes were about?" Hank adjusted the earphone in his right ear.

"They are requests for money." I flipped my hair over my shoulder to get it away from my ear so I could fit the earpiece in properly. Hank took a look at it. "Sally Ann said Judie told her people were like ants, coming out of the woodwork."

"I bet. What a shame." Jerry tsked. "Everyone ready?"

"Yep," Hank and I both agreed before all three of us went our separate ways.

I had decided to stay back in the barn so I could take a look at the foals. One of them could grow up to be a Kentucky Derby winner. They were so cute on their skinny legs that would soon be so full of bulging muscles.

"You keep eating that grass," I told one of them when I walked by. He was munching on some of our Kentucky bluegrass that was full of limestone, minerals, and all the things that supposedly fed our horses so well to make them the best.

I found Judie Doughty in the very back stall in her ball gown, talking to a young woman about my age, who was not dressed for the fundraiser, and another young woman who had on a skirt suit and held a folio close to her chest.

"You must be Mae." Judie put her hand out. "I'm Judie."

"Nice to meet you in person." I took her hand and gave it a good shake. "Who is this?" I was asking about the foal, but instead she introduced me to the horse trainer.

"This is Delaney Harrison. She's my horse trainer for all the horses, and she looks after the foundation horses." Judie held up a finger when an older man walked up and got her attention, taking her off to the side.

I couldn't help but notice the man and Judie walked into the stall next to us. Before I could ask about the other lady, she walked off with the man.

"It's nice to meet you." I watched Delaney brush the foal before someone else came in, took it by the bridle, and guided it out of the stall and down the barn. "What exactly do you do for Judie?"

"I train all of her horses as well as check out potential foals for this fundraiser. I guess it's the first time she's done it, but from what I understand, she's going to keep doing it." Delaney picked up around the stall, putting brushes and tools in buckets.

There was a ruckus coming from the stall next door.

"This is the one." The woman's voice carried through the stall walls. "She will be the one to bring the most money, and this is the one you need to focus on. Do you understand me?"

Faintly I could hear Judie trying to talk to the woman, but Delaney was so loud, it was hard for me to hear.

One thing I did hear clearly was the woman Judie was talking to almost threatening her.

"I'll make darn sure that word got around how Judie was a scam artist, and the foundation would go under," I heard her murmur in a very loud, hushed tone.

"What exactly do you do to check out foals?" I stopped eavesdropping and asked Delaney the question. This had nothing to do with the investigation. I just found it interesting, and I wanted to stick around to see who was next door.

"This year after she won—um, came into some money, we went looking for what I'd call the class-B breeders. Not the top of the line and not the bottom of the barrel. Ones that had potential to be great racehorses that didn't have the perfect breeding stock." It was all about genetics when it came to horse breeding. "Spring is when most foals are born, so the fall is the perfect time to get them sold and start training. That's why she picked August."

"Did any of the bottom-of-the-barrel owners try to get in on the action?" I asked, thinking that if Judie had shunned one, then maybe they would write her threatening letters.

"There were several people upset, but it's business." She picked up a bucket in each hand and started out the stall door. "Everyone thinks their horse is going to be the next Triple Crown winner." She pointed to the stall where the arguing was coming from. "Ashley Marzullo for one. She thinks her foal should start out at twenty thousand dollars. I told Judie Ashley's foal wasn't worth but eight thousand. Ashley's foal wasn't even in the auction until late this afternoon. Who knows how Ashley got in, but Judie insisted."

"Who was the guy who came in and got Judie?" I asked.

"Powell Doughty, Judie's husband," she said and walked out of the barn, leaving me there to wonder how I could get my hands on the list of class-B clients and the names of the owners that were mad about not getting in on the auction.

What did Powell know? Was he part of his wife's fundraiser? Did he have as much interest in the horses as she did?

"And the other lady with Judie?" I asked about the woman with the folio.

"Judie's shadow?" Delaney laughed. "No joke. That's Iona Thatcher. She's Judie's assistant. It's a joke around here that she even goes to the bathroom with Judie, might even clean Judie up afterwards, if you know what I mean."

I walked out of the barn and around to the ring, where I noticed they were actually walking the foals, letting them trot and build up a little tension in their muscles, the sweat making them more defined, before they led them up to another barn on the Old Train Station property where they paraded the foals in front of a crowd with bidding paddles in their hands.

Coke had really outdone herself with the decorating. It was a perfect time of the night, and she took full advantage of it by placing light lanterns all around the property, including the paths from the motel to each barn and where each event was being held.

She had a couple of nice lakes, and she'd taken advantage of those by placing floating lanterns in the water. The reflection of the lantern lights in the water created a magical glow as the lanterns floated.

The auctioneer voice trailed out of the barn they were using for the auction. He spoke so fast I couldn't even begin to understand what he was saying over the loud microphone. The only time I'd really gotten a few goose bumps was when one of the foals had gone up for auction and the highest bidder was denied.

"You can't deny me!" The man's boisterous voice echoed through the air and bounced off the mountains. "I've got good money, and I won!"

"Stand by," Jerry called in my earpiece.

Out of the corner of my eye, I saw Hank swiftly moving up the right side of the barn and Jerry heading up the left, so I took the middle.

"I'm not letting you take this from me, Judie!" The man held his fist in the air.

"I'm sorry, sir." The auctioneer pointed his gavel at the man just as the man started to charge up to the podium.

Iona Thatcher walked up on the small stage, which was big enough for just the auctioneer and his podium where he called the auction. She handed him a piece of paper then walked off.

Hank made it there before the man could take another step. Hank put a firm palm on the man's chest and gave him a hard stare as though he was daring the man to even try to get past him.

My toes tingled seeing Hank in action. He was so good at his job.

"The fine print reads clearly that Judie can decline the highest bid." The auctioneer turned the paper around. "I do believe this is your name and paddle number."

The man shoved Hank's hand off of him.

"I swear I'll make sure your name is mud in this business," the man snarled at Judie before he turned to exit the barn.

The auctioneer finished calling all the foals, and to my relief, there wasn't another incident. It didn't take long for everyone to leave the outside ring where the auction took place and head into the barn to finish out the fundraiser with food, dancing, cocktails, and good conversation.

"Stuffed mushroom?" A person with a familiar voice shoved a tray full of fancy-looking mushrooms in my face.

"Queenie!" I was shocked to see her. "What are you doing here?"

"It's not just me." She pointed to the catering counter, where Dottie, Betts, and Abby were picking up trays to carry around for bidders to munch on. "Coke had mentioned to Betts when Betts was here cleaning the rooms earlier that she needed a few people to help with the catered part of the auction. You weren't around when she called everyone, and Dottie told us that you were doing some sort of undercover investigating here. How could you not include us?"

"I would, but I'm not even sure what I'm trying to find." I loved having my friends here. It made it so much easier. "So what if I tell you, and you tell the girls?"

It was a no-brainer situation to be in. The Laundry Club Ladies and I had solved so many cases before, and we worked well together. They were just as good, if not better, at finding clues as I was.

"And there's no dead bodies." I was happy to tell Queenie how we were just on a fact-finding spree and not some murder scene.

"No, but that one guy who lost the highest bid sure was mad." Queenie took one of the mushrooms off the tray and ate it.

"Yeah. That was crazy." I was glad to see he wasn't in the barn.

"I ran into him. Literally." Queenie took another mushroom and told me all about it. "I was walking out of the Caboose Diner after I'd gotten the tray, since all the food is being funneled out there. When I opened the door to come here, he wasn't looking, and neither was I. We almost got covered in these little babies." She laughed and popped the mushroom into her mouth. "He was fussing and saying how he was going to get Judie one way or another, before he disappeared into one of the motel rooms."

Queenie was more than happy to let Abby, Dottie, and Betts know what was going on and to keep their ear to the ground about Judie winning the lottery and potential people who might have an interest.

The earpieces were pretty quiet. Hank, Jerry, and I passed each other a few times during the auction and up in the other barn, where Coke had everything set up for the big celebratory part of the evening.

Blue Ethel and the Adolescent Farm Boys were on the stage in the front of the barn, Ty Randal was behind the buffet and slicing up roast beef and ham, while the Laundry Club Ladies continued to take the trays of finger foods around.

Guests had their phones out, taking photos and recording everyone having fun.

The night was getting started off with a bang, a literal bang as soon as Judie stood up on stage at the microphone with Powell on one side and their son, Evan, on the other. She gave a brief welcome and talked a little bit about the fundraiser.

Coke Ogden opened the slider doors behind the band. It was an area she liked to use for weddings when couples set off fireworks in the field beyond the barn. The mountains made a gorgeous backdrop and added to the ambiance.

"Hank! Judie!" I screamed when I noticed a red dot in the center of Judie's forehead before the first set of fireworks zoomed up into the sky, giving off a loud boom.

Hank was closest to the stage. He bolted up the steps and tackled Judie to the ground. As I made my way up to the stage, I noticed Coke had run over to the electric panel to turn on the lights.

A collective gasp came over the guests as they all looked at the dance floor.

Ashley Marzullo's body lay lifeless with blood trickling away from her head. She'd danced her last dance.

CHAPTER EIGHT

"Fancy seeing you here." Tucker Pyle had showed up right before Sheriff Al Hemmer had gotten on the scene.

Hank and Jerry had taken over after the shots rang out and cleared the dance floor, careful not to hurt any evidence. Hank had also rounded up Judie and her family, settling them at one of the bourbon barrel tables in the barn because he knew Al would want to question them.

"It's not that unusual," Al Hemmer noted. "I guess we will start with you since you seem to know more than the law." Al directed his comment to me as I stood there with Hank and Jerry. "What's happened here, Mae?"

Jerry cut in, "Let me explain. Mine and Hank's private investigation services were hired by Judie Doughty due to some life-threatening letters she'd received. Tonight Hank and I were keeping an eye out for Judie, and Mae was just gathering some information." Before Al had gotten there, Jerry had gone out to his car and gotten the case file with all the letters in it. "Since I know this is now a homicide and the sheriff's department, along with the rangers, will take over, I will hand these over to you."

"You mean you aren't going to keep working for me?" Judie jumped to her feet. "Someone tried to kill me."

"How do you know it was you and not the victim?" Al asked.

"I saw the red laser pointed on her forehead." I spoke up. "That's when I yelled, 'Hank,' and he jumped on stage to tackle her."

"The intended target was on stage, but the bullet got the victim on the dance floor in front of the stage?" Tucker looked around. He left the question hanging there and began to walk out of the barn, opposite the stage.

I followed him.

"Tell me exactly what you saw." Tucker and I walked side by side.

"Judie was giving a speech while Coke opened the door behind the stage." I touched Tucker's arm. "When Coke opened the door, I noticed the laser pointing at Judie's head, so while everyone was watching the stage and what was going on behind the stage, the killer was in the back of the barn. They shot and hit Ashley."

We stopped at the fence between the back of the barn and the field where the fireworks had gone off, getting a look at the entire guts of the barn.

Al Hemmer walked up.

"I reckon you better tell me what's goin' on." Al indicated by the motion of his head that he was all ears.

"I'm not sure what Hank and Jerry told you, but they asked me to listen around about anyone who would've sent Judie Doughty threatening letters." And by listen around, Al knew I meant snooping. "I started by going to the places she had gone to see if she made any comments to them, or if the owners had seen anyone suspicious around."

I glanced past Al's shoulder. Judie's family and Delaney Harrison were crowded around her.

"I went to see Helen Pyle because Judie had gone there to get her hair done this morning as well as her nails." I wasn't sure how much detail Al wanted, but I gave him the basics. "The only thing Sally Ann told me that I found of interest was Judie did confide in her that she'd won the lottery and that people were coming out of the woodwork, asking for money." There was a little scurrying going on inside of the barn, and I shifted my focus to see what was happening.

"I'll go check." Tucker excused himself.

"I also asked Coke if she'd seen anything out of the ordinary, and nothing. Just the same people Judie surrounded herself with, like her husband, son, horse trainer, and Iona." I watched Tucker walking over to Judie's group and didn't see Iona, which I found odd since Delaney had told me Iona never left Judie's side.

I kept that little bit of information to myself in hopes Hank would let me know they were still going to stay on Judie's case.

It would be someone to check out.

"Are you okay?" Hank asked in my ear.

"Mm-hmm," I hummed so Al wouldn't notice me talking with Hank through my earpiece.

"Good. Keep Al talking because I'm searching around for evidence while they take Judie into the house. She's going to take some medication and go to bed." Hank clicked out of my ear. "Judie has upped our payday, so this would be a good cut for all of us."

Tucker and Judie, along with her entourage, exited the far end of the barn. I kept an eye on Al and an eye on Hank, who was casually talking to many of the deputies he'd worked with before.

"I was standing at the side of the barn when Judie was up on stage, um, eating." I decided to filter in some gibberish side talk to keep Al here. "Did you try those delicious finger foods Ty made for the event?"

"No." Al shook his head and looked up from his little notepad.

"They were delicious. I'm telling you that you need to tell your mama to get Ty to make her some of those little finger thingies."

Al looked up at me. "My mama is a good cook." He was trying to really focus on his notes. "What else did you see?"

"I saw Dottie, Betts, and Queenie here too. Even Abby. Her and Bobby Ray are so happy." I let out a long sigh.

"I mean when the fireworks rang out. You're the one who yelled out to Hank, so you had to have seen something." Al tried to bring me back to his investigation.

"Hank. I did yell Hank." I elbowed Al. "Between me and you, I'm thrilled Hank is back. I am so in love that I just can't stand it."

"I'm happy for you." Al's eyes narrowed. "Are you okay? You need to see a doctor? Someone you can talk to?"

"No. Why?" I asked.

"Maybe you've seen one too many dead people and you need to talk to someone, because you're acting weird." Al was catching on to my rambling. "I just need to know about the attempt to kill Judie."

"So you have decided Ashley was just at the wrong place at the wrong time?" I questioned.

"From what I understand, you noticed a laser pointed at Judie, and when you yelled for Hank, he bolted up to the stage and tackled her down. I think Ashley turned around and got into the line of fire, which was how she got killed."

Al surprised me. He'd not been the best choice for sheriff, but he'd really stepped up to the plate.

"I think that sounds about right." I was impressed, even though his theory was the logical one anyone would've come up with.

"Did you notice anyone run out of the barn? Leave the barn?" Al asked.

"No. Coke Ogden caught my eye when she flipped on the lights. That's when I heard everyone gasping and saw Ashley's body on the floor." As I told him the facts, I recalled who was on stage when the shot rang out.

"Hey, anything new?" Hank walked up and asked Al.

"No, but thank you for all of your work. The Normal sheriff's department really appreciates all the information you and Jerry gave us." Al seemed to be telling Hank that it was their job now and that we should go.

"You're welcome." Hank unbuttoned the tuxedo jacket, took it off, and flung it over his shoulder. "I guess we will be going now."

"I'll be in touch." Al's eyes were sharp. "And congrats on you two getting back together. That's great. It's good to hear how happy Mae is."

"Thanks, man." Hank smiled and looked at me.

"Whoever fired the shot had to have known when the fireworks were going off," I muttered under my breath as Hank and I walked off. "Down to the minute, the shooter knew."

"And did you notice it was before the fundraiser amount was actually announced?" Hank might've had an important clue. "The breeder has time to pull out the foal until the final numbers are in. Which I wonder if a breeder didn't get enough of a threshold to sell the foal?"

"Which tells me that I really need to get my hands on that donor list." I thought back to what Delaney had told me. "The trainer told me there were a lot of horse breeders who wanted to participate in auctioning off their foals. They are classified by their breeding status, and Judie doesn't allow anyone with low status to go into the auction."

"Then the shooter could've been someone who didn't make the cut to have in a foal and was angry at Judie for classifying their breeding that way." Hank finished my thought.

We walked through the field away from the barns and up to the Old Train Station Motel, stopping briefly to look back at the crime scene. Jerry Truman was still in the circle, talking to his old group of deputies, no doubt rubbing elbows to keep the lines of communication open to help aid in our investigation.

"When you get a reputation in the horse business that you're not breeding quality stock, you have no income." I turned the motive into money. "And if no one really knew Judie had won the lottery, it probably isn't about the lottery. But Sally Ann did say Judie had been getting letters from people she didn't know or hadn't seen in a long time who had heard she won the lottery."

"Which is it?" Hank asked. We walked through the courtyard and out to the parking lot to our cars. "You want to let people know you won the lottery or not? Who did she tell and why? Whoever she did tell ended up telling people, if what she said about the letters is right."

"I want to see the letters," I said.

"Yeah, me too." Hank opened the door of my Focus. "Are you really happy?"

"What?" I lowered my gaze in confusion.

"What Al said. He said you were really happy that I'm back, and you've not told me that." He laughed as if he were severely amused. "Your lips tell me you're happy, but I've not heard it with my ears."

"I don't know." I shrugged and got in the car. "I guess you're going to have to court me to find out."

"Mm-hmm." His smile turned into an irresistibly devastating grin before he shut my door and walked over to his truck.

I started up the car and drove out of the parking lot and down Fawn Road, with Hank's headlights not too far behind me. Every curve I took, his lights disappeared, and it took a few seconds before they'd come back.

The moon hung down over the wide-open country road until I made it past downtown, where I wound the car through the curves with only my headlights to guide me. The darkness lay ahead, and I knew if I went one inch to the right or left of the shoulder, my car could plunge over the steep cliff, and off to my death I'd be.

Poor Ashley Marzullo. My thoughts had wandered to the moment Coke had flipped on all the lights inside of the barn. Seeing the young woman lying there made me think about all the things I knew about her.

She had money. She was particular about her foal. She had been accepted late to the auction for the fundraiser and wanted more money than Judie was going to give.

"Twenty thousand dollars," I repeated the number Ashley had given Judie for the start of her bid. "What did the foal go for?"

There was a little doubt in our theory that the hit was on Judie. I called Hank from the car's hands-free phone.

"Miss me already?" Hank's southern drawl echoed through my car speakers. "I'm right behind you."

"No. Yes. I mean, yes, I miss you, but that's not why I'm calling." I found it to be funny how Hank had no real idea how I worked while sleuthing for clues. So I told him, "When I think of a new idea or theory when I'm checking into details, I begin to write those down. But now that we are working together, I thought I'd call."

"Dang. That busts my bubble. Go on."

"When I was talking to Delaney in the barn, I overheard Ashley upset in the stall with the foal she had there for the auction. She told Judie she wanted the bidding to start at twenty thousand dollars. According to Delaney, the foal wasn't worth that much, and Ashley had gotten accepted into the fundraising auction at the last minute." I slowed down when I got to the last hairpin curve that was before the turnoff to the gravel drive that wound back into the woods where Happy Trails Campground was located.

The only thing that told you a campground was located there was an old wooden archway with Happy Trails Campground carved into it.

"You're saying the hit could've actually been on Ashley and not Judie?" Hank did it again. Finished my thought. "What about the laser on Judie's head?"

"That I don't know." I noodled the fact. "Maybe Ashley wasn't the intended target, but she did have a beef with Judie."

CHAPTER NINE

As the manager of Happy Trails Campground, there were only so many things Dottie Swaggert could do when she was working. She was excellent about inputting all the data from the guests and the payments into the system, keeping the calendar of events up to date, and making sure all the guests had what they needed while they stayed.

We offered various themed baskets for the guests, from ones centered around celebrating special occasions to items they might've forgotten at home. They were at an extra cost, and the money for those went to keeping the vending machines stocked over at the recreational building, where the games and washing machines were located.

Dottie also oversaw all the vending machines and kept the games in good condition.

I had the task of doing all the yucky things like budgeting and making sure profits were put back into the campground. After it was all said and done, I only had enough money to pay Dottie and Henry their salaries. There wasn't much I needed, since I lived here. So I paid myself food money, and that was pretty much about it.

"Good morning," I answered my cell phone the next morning while sitting at the office desk since it was my turn to open. It was Mary Elizabeth calling.

"I was making some breakfast casseroles for the bed-and-breakfast guests and thought of how much you used to love waking up on a weekend morning with the smell wafting through our house." Mary Elizabeth was always so good at remembering the details that made her house a home. "I made an extra one for you. I'll bring it to book club tonight."

"Oh, gosh. I forgot all about book club." I glanced over at the wipe-off board that had not only the calendar of events, which the guests could come check out to see what was going on around Normal and the campground, but my own personal agenda, which was pretty nonexistent.

"I reckon you did. Seeing how I hear you've been occupied with Hank Sharp coming back into town." Mary Elizabeth was ready for the gossip.

"I did miss him." I wasn't quite ready to tell her about how many times I'd rolled over last night and peeked out the campervan bedroom window to look down at Hank's camper. "And he really seems to be embracing the real me."

It was all I was going to say, because I'd bet Mary Elizabeth already had the hope chest out that she'd been collecting for since I showed up on her doorstep with the foster counselor when I was a kid.

"We can talk about that later." To be fair to Hank, I wasn't sure where we stood, as we hadn't gotten to discuss that yet, and I kinda liked having the feelings to myself for a little while.

Around here, once your feelings or relationship was known, it was on display for the entire town to see.

The door of the office opened. It was Bobby Ray. I waved him in.

"Is that Mary Elizabeth?" he mouthed.

I nodded.

"Don't tell her I'm here." His eyes were big as he waved both hands in front of him.

"Thank you in advance for the casserole. I'll get it at book club," I told her, eager to get off the phone so I could talk to Bobby Ray about his thoughts on his birth mother.

We'd yet to get a chance to talk about it, since I'd hightailed it out of the get-together after Hank's phone call about him being back and parked in the campground.

"All right. I was just calling to make sure you were going to be there, so I'll see you later." Mary Elizabeth and I said our goodbyes.

"What was all the sneaking around about?" I shifted gears. I hit the save button on the budget spreadsheet and eased back from the desk to give Bobby Ray my full attention.

"She's been all over me about Nina's money request." His temper started to bubble right at the surface. "She didn't tell you?"

"No. This is the first I've heard of it." I knew this was one of the things Mary Elizabeth had been worried about after she'd heard Bobby Ray had found his birth mother.

"Nina has gone from job to job. She's not been able to pay her bills and owes a lot of money to past landlords and debts." His face clouded with uneasiness. "It's so hard to talk about, Mae. To put my feelings in words. I think I'm worrying Abby to death because she keeps asking what's in my head, and I have this guilt."

"I'm sorry." I was so glad he felt like he could come to me. There'd been so many times I'd called on him to talk about the guilt I had surrounding my family's death. I'd kept Mary Elizabeth at a good safe distance from my heart in fear I'd been disloyal to my own mother. "What is the guilt over?"

"I guess I feel like I should give her the money, but then again, I can only wonder if she did decide to meet me because she needed money. I really think my guilt is me not trusting her." He looked down at his hands. They'd hadn't become all black with grease yet since it was still morning.

By the end of the day, he'd be a big grease pit from head to toe from his work underneath the hoods of cars.

"Trust is very important in a relationship, and it does take time." I was careful about giving advice. I sure didn't want to give the wrong advice for fear he'd get mad at me in the end. "It might not take you long to trust, but I know that I'm pretty leery. Not that Hank and I are in the same situation, but it does come down to trust. Can I trust who this new Hank is? Does he really want to make a future? Has he changed his mind about children if we ever cross that path?"

"The thing with Hank is that he's always been the same. The Hank he is today is the Hank he is without that job that made him stay away from home. The job where day in and day out he had to deal with criminals. I'm not saying the new job as private investigator doesn't deal with criminals; it's just not keeping him from the things he loves." Bobby Ray grinned. "May-bell-ine, you sure did make that boy's heart turn to mush."

CHAPTER TEN

As much as I'd like to say I'd helped Bobby Ray, I knew **deep in my** heart he wasn't there for advice. He needed an ear to listen as he talked out his own issues. Bobby Ray acted tough on the exterior, but he was as soft as he said Hank was, and he had a good heart.

My mind was preoccupied with Bobby Ray for most of the morning, even when Fifi and I went for our midmorning walk around the campground to check on the guests.

"I guess." I talked to her like she was human when she ran over to Hank's camper. "Chester? Wanna come play?" I hollered out before I even got to the camper door. I fiddled with all the keys on the keyring to find Hank's then realized the camper wasn't the same.

If I knew Hank—and I knew Hank—he probably didn't even have the door locked.

Chester was waiting at the door when I popped it open. It was supposed to be an easy "open the door and let him run out," but I couldn't help but notice the mess of papers all over the camper floor. Hank Sharp was a very tidy man. He liked to keep everything neat, and that included all of his paperwork.

I'd never seen such a mess in my life. I stepped up into the camper and noticed there were bite marks on the papers.

"It doesn't take a sleuth to figure out who made this mess," I told myself and started to pick up the pieces of paper. "Huh," I said in a curious way when I noticed these were pieces of paper from his Mammoth Cave post.

It wasn't like I could just close my eyes and pick up the papers, nor stop myself from reading them as I did.

This was clearly a murder case about a man by the name of Walter Adams, but I wasn't sure why Hank had the file. If he was done with his post from Mammoth Cave, then why was the paperwork still here?

"Take your own words, Mae," I said to myself and gathered up all the papers, putting them back on the table where I was sure Chester had gotten ahold of them. "Trust. I bet he just forgot to turn in all his files, that's all."

Why on earth was I questioning things Hank had in his camper? Instead of leaving, like I should've, I walked around to look at the new camper. It wasn't brand-new, but it was new for him and for me.

It was much nicer than the one he'd had and had a cool bump-out with two leather chairs that faced a gas fireplace and a mounted TV. Immediately I began to envision the two of us relaxing after a long day of hiking with a big bowl of popcorn while binge-watching something on that big television.

Distant barking brought me out of my head. I headed out of the camper. Dottie Swaggert looked like a freight train with the cigarette smoke billowing behind her as she walked down the road toward me. She still had on her green satin pajamas, and pink foam curlers were clipped all over her red hair. Her matching fuzzy slippers carried her lanky five-foot-nine frame as fast as her hips would let her go.

"Maybelline! Maybelline!" She waved her hands. "I was going to wake you up last night, but I wasn't sure where you'd be." She leaned over a smidgen and glanced past my shoulder at Hank's camper. "Anyways, there was some guy here yesterday morning asking about you and Hank. He seemed awfully suspicious to me, so I told him I didn't know a thing about you two since y'all broke up, and then he asked if I'd seen Hank."

"He did?" I wondered who on earth it could be.

"Yep, sure did." She took a long draw of her cigarette. The tip was like a heartbeat. The longer she sucked, the longer it turned bright red before it slowly faded, waiting for the next inhale. "I didn't say a word. It was odd."

"Do you think it had to do with Ashley Marzullo's murder? Or better yet, Judie's attempted murder?" It was something we had to look at from all angles.

"That's what I was thinkin'." Dottie tapped her temple with the hand holding the smoke. I cringed when I noticed she got a little too close to the pink sponge on the curler.

She would catch her hair on fire, and it wouldn't be the first time she'd set something ablaze with a cigarette.

"Good. If he comes back, don't say a word." I wasn't really sure what Hank's policy on giving out information on his and Jerry's cases was, but I knew one thing for sure. When he was with the sheriff's department, he kept things tight to the cuff.

"Now that I'm up, I figured I'd get ready for the day. I'll go on to work, and you can do whatever it is you need to do." She waved her hand at me.

"I do have to go into town and meet with Jerry and Hank to discuss what happened at the fundraiser and what we are doing next. Plus I need to stop by the Cookie Crumble." I forgot how I'd signed up to bring a dessert for the book club, but it was easily solved by going to see our friend Christine Watson, who just so happened to make the best cookies in the world.

"It sounds to me like you better get going if you're going to make it on time for book club. But first I want to know what exactly is Hank Sharp's intentions?" She quirked her eyebrow questioningly.

"I don't know. I think he really wants to get back together, and I'm willing to give him that chance." The tone of my voice was echoed by the smile on my face. "Oh, Dottie. I really missed him, and now that he's not in any type of law enforcement, he really is embracing my ways, which makes me believe that we can work together."

"What about kids?" Dottie asked the important question that actually caused the original breakup we'd not recovered from.

"He said that he's open to it now that he's not in harm's way and not working long, crazy hours." Chester and Fifi ran up to us. "Let's get you two back home."

Chester and Fifi darted up to my camper while Dottie and I walked behind them.

"He's hotter than donut grease with that beard." Dottie gave me a reassuring smile with one of her crazy sayings that told me she was in support of me.

"There certainly ain't nothing wrong with your eyes." I laughed and thanked her for working earlier so I could head on over to Trails Coffee, where I found Hank and Jerry already going over the clues.

Gert Hobson had given them an unlimited supply of her fall-blend coffee. It was like a cozy hug with each sip. Even though the weather hadn't fully turned, this blend was one of my favorites.

"Can I get y'all anything else?" Gert asked.

"I don't know how you do it, but this year's blend is better than last's." I held the mug between my hands and lifted it up to my nose. I took a deep breath in and a long sigh out.

"I do too. I think this year I was able to use a swirl of natural pumpkin along with the cinnamon and nutmeg flavors to really bring out the creamy comfort of autumn and what it would taste like if you could put it in a warm mug." She really did take her coffee roasting to a whole different level of art form.

Even how she talked made me feel all gooey and cozy inside.

"I'll be in the coffee shop if you need a refill." She walked out, leaving me, Hank, and Jerry alone.

"Obviously the plan has changed from trying to figure out who sent Judie the threatening letters to who tried to kill Judie." Jerry reiterated what they'd written on a huge piece of clear plastic that was new since yesterday.

An excitement mixed with fear quivered through me. The way Jerry had everything set up today looked like a real investigation room.

"Mae, Hank and I have talked about what you could do since this is now a homicide and Judie has given us even more money to figure this out."

I didn't like what I was hearing.

"Why can't I just be part of the team?" I asked.

"You don't need to be worried with all of this." Jerry looked at the board. "You have a life. You have Happy Trails Campground to run, but we would still like for you to keep your ear to the ground."

"I think Mae will be okay." Hank gave me a reassuring look. "I know we talked, but there's nothing we are doing today that'll put her in any danger."

"If you say so." Jerry's mouth set in annoyance, as if he didn't like that Hank had gone back on what they'd discussed before I got there.

"If it's any interest, I've come up with some ideas." I grabbed my bag and pulled out my notebook. "We need a list of the horse owners in the auction as well as the ones who were turned down by Judie. I think we could have a possible motive of hurt and feelings of being left out due to the way not being included could harm a reputation. We all know that these large farms rely on great reputations of good horse breeding, and if Judie has begun to classify breeding to her own standards, this could take several farms out of the horse game."

Jerry liked what I said because he wrote it on the big plastic board under possible motives.

"There were so many guests, and a lot of them had their video calls on because some of the people bidding were represented by people who couldn't be there in person. There were also a lot of people videotaping Judie speaking right before the fireworks went off. We need to get the guest list and see if we can look at people's footage." I knew this was going to take time, but Jerry wrote it down.

"I think this is something Al Hemmer will do, but I can ask Granny." Hank referred to his granny, Agnes Swift, who was the dispatch operator for the Normal sheriff's department.

"Oh. I'd love to see her. I'll go by there." I couldn't wait to hear what she thought about Hank being in town.

"That's okay. I can do it. I'd love to see her," Hank insisted. I didn't bother to change his mind because I knew how close they were since she practically raised him.

"That's good." Jerry wrote that down. "What about her family?"

"Well, they did seem very supportive of her, but I wonder what the inheritance situation looked like. Did her son get anything? Was her winning the lottery a good reason for him to kill her? In these cases, the husband has been known to kill for hire." I sounded like one of those television-show detectives.

"I thought about that, so I already did some digging into her finances, but nothing noticeable has turned up yet." He wrote down his duties. "I will go see her today and clear some things up."

"I'd like to talk to her too." There was a way I had with people, and especially women. I knew if I could talk to her alone, I'd be able to get some information about possible people who didn't like her, even though she'd claimed everyone liked her.

"What about the guy who was bidding on the foal, and Judie had to make the decision for his farm not to win with the highest bid?" I questioned.

"I looked into that one." Jerry shuffled some papers on his desk. "There's a clause, small print, but it's there." He handed me the paper. "I've got awful eyes. Can you read that out loud?"

"Sure." I took the paper. "If for any reason Judie Doughty believes the highest bidder is not fit to take proper care of the foal, Judie has the right to decline the offer." I looked down the paper at the signature. "It's signed."

"Yeah, but he did say he was going to make sure her name was mud." Hank was right. If anyone had a public fight with Judie that night, it was that guy.

"Queenie told me she saw him going into a room at the Old Train Station. He must be staying there, so I'd like to talk to him too." My list of people to see was growing. "She said he was fussing and saying how he was going to get Judie one way or another."

Jerry grabbed his keys. "I say we head on over there to see if he's still there."

Jerry didn't need to say anything else. We bolted out the door.

CHAPTER ELEVEN

I nstead of us riding together out to the Old Train Station Motel, we drove separately. Hank said he was going to see Agnes at the department about the phone footage after we checked out the man at the hotel, while Jerry was going to get back on looking into Judie's financials.

Me, I was going to snoop around the motel for a while and see if I could talk to Judie or even get in front of Iona, her right hand, to pick her brain about what had taken place, or even just if she knew anyone who had motive to pull the trigger.

Then I would have enough time to go to the Cookie Crumble and grab the desserts before I headed back into downtown to meet for book club at the Laundry Club.

"Can I get y'all a fresh glass of sweet tea?" Coke asked after me, Jerry, and Hank had entered the Caboose Diner. She was standing at the counter, talking to a few people.

I noticed the interim preacher from the Normal Baptist Church sitting in a booth with Judie's son, Evan.

"Odd, ain't it?" Coke gave the snide remark when she saw me stare a moment too long. "He came in here this morning asking if we had any clergy around for him to talk to." Coke disappeared into the kitchen to get the tea.

"That's strange. Why would Evan want to see a preacher who he doesn't know?" Jerry asked.

"Guilt. Clean a guilty mind." Without even saying any more, I knew this put Evan on the suspect list.

"I really need to get a good look into those financials." Jerry tapped his finger on the counter. There was some silence between us as if we were mulling over what we were witnessing and our thoughts were coming together. "Hey, Coke." Jerry got her attention as she set down all of our teas. "What room is Judie Doughty staying in?"

"Number two." She threw a chin. "Her boy is in number six. The trainer and assistant are in number eight."

"I'm also looking for the man who got really upset at the auction. Do you remember him?" I asked. "Queenie said she saw him going into a room after Judie took his highest bid away."

"Angus Coo. He's in room five. It's the only room with a side entrance to the courtyard since it's on the corner." She shook her head. "He hasn't left his room since he went in there. I knocked on his door to see if I could bring him something to eat. He didn't open it. He mumbled something, and I let him be. He's supposed to be checking out today."

"Thanks." I took a drink of the tea. "I say we go see him before he gets out of town."

The three of us stood up, but not before I made eye contact with the preacher. I knew Mary Elizabeth had had him over for supper one night, so I made a mental note to talk to her about him at book club.

Instead of going to the front of the motel, we went to the side door of motel room five, where Coke said Angus Coo was staying. Hank curled in his middle finger and used his knuckle to knock on the door right below the brass number five hanging in the middle.

We stood back and waited a minute or so before Hank knocked again, using all of his knuckles from his fisted hand.

After waiting another minute, Hank looked back at me and Jerry. He said, "Do you think he's in the shower?"

Jerry and I shrugged.

Jerry stepped in front of Hank and literally beat on the door before he put his ear up to the door.

"I hear something like talking." He looked back at us.

"I'll go around to the front. Maybe the window shades are pulled." I headed around the corner where all of the doors to each room were lined up one after the other, starting with number five and proceeding down to room ten. The opposite side of the courtyard was where rooms number one through four were located.

The window shades were pulled closed, and when I went to knock on the door, I noticed the door was cracked.

"Hank! Jerry!" I called out to get them to join me.

"What?" Jerry made it around the corner first, and close by was Hank.

"The door is cracked, and I think what you heard was the television." I took a step back, knowing I wasn't armed like the two of them. If they wanted to open the door and find this Angus guy on the other end of a gun and not the receiving end, I didn't want to be the one to get shot.

"Angus? I'm Jerry." Jerry pushed open the door. "Aww, man." Jerry's voice turned raspy. He leaned on the doorjamb and gave a head tilt, indicating for Hank to look.

"What?" I asked when I noticed Hank's eye bulge and his inability to blink.

"Someone got to him before we did." Hank shoved the door open fully, letting the last bit of the day's sunlight filter in on Agnus Coo's body.

A pool of blood was around his head.

CHAPTER TWELVE

"There's a note." Al Hemmer had come out to the courtyard, where we were waiting to be interviewed by him or one of the Normal sheriff's deputies. "Apparently he accidentally shot Ashley Marzullo when he was aiming for Judie Doughty."

He handed Hank the plastic evidence bag with the note inside, fully open so it could be read.

Jerry and I stood behind Hank to read the letter as Hank read it.

"He claims he was going to kill Judie because if he didn't come back with that foal to the farm, his job was going to be terminated. He'd planned on killing her and himself, but after what he'd done to Ashley, he couldn't bring himself to be caught for her death, so he just went ahead and ended it." Hank summarized the note. "Death by poison."

"He didn't shoot himself?" I wondered about the pool of blood.

"Nope. Nose and mouth bleeding was the source of the blood. Looks like this is a closed case." Al seemed pretty pleased with himself even though he technically didn't solve it. "The shell casing found in the barn last night matches the gun found in Mr. Coo's room."

"Where's the gun?" Jerry asked. "I'd like to see it."

"We've collected it in evidence. Once it's processed and we have confirmed it is the same weapon, we will let you know so you can tell your client everything is all good and she's safe. No more threats." Al excused himself.

"This can't be right." I couldn't wrap my head around the note Angus left. "Why didn't he just shoot himself? Why go through the hassle of taking some sort of poison only to die that way?"

"No man would do that." Hank slid his gaze to Jerry.

"You're right. A man would just shoot. And from the looks of it, there didn't appear to be any forced entry, which makes me wonder who he knew at his door." I couldn't help but make the observation.

"Did you notice there were two glasses on the small table?" Hank had such a good eye for detail even when there was very little time to take things in.

"This isn't as closed tight as Al thinks, but"—Jerry put his hands out as if he were dampening the situation—"we will keep this close to our vest and continue to look around. Besides, we still don't have the culprit who sent Judie those letters."

Tucker Pyle walked into the courtyard and motioned for me to come talk to him.

"What's he want?" Hank took a tone.

"Not sure." I got up. "I'll be right back."

I wasn't sure, but I thought Hank felt either a bit jealous or intimidated by Tucker, though he had no reason to be. Later I'd make sure Hank was okay, but I wanted to see what Tucker knew.

"I wanted you to know that we got some footage from one of the fundraiser's guests. They were standing outside of the barn, filming the full moon while Judie was talking. They continued to video after the fireworks went off, and it shows a guy running from the barn right after the first round of fireworks went off. I ran it through some recognition software and got an initial hit on this well-known gun for hire. Shaw Mole is his name." Tucker took out his phone and showed me a photo.

"Shaw Mole?" I rolled my eyes.

"He's like a mole. Comes in at night. No one sees him, but he leaves all sorts of destruction afterwards." Tucker shook his head. "Anyways, we've got an APB out on him. It's gone statewide and soon to go out to the surrounding states. Unfortunately, like most state parks, it's so vast that he could be here anywhere."

"Thanks for the info." I knew this would be great information to take back to Hank and Jerry. "Do you think he killed Angus Coo? Supposedly he died by poison suicide."

Both of us stopped talking when Coroner Colonel Holz rolled the church cart past us. Colonel stopped briefly to wave at Hank and Jerry before he proceeded to room five.

"Something seems awfully fishy." Tucker grabbed Al when Al started to walk past us. "We have a shooter."

"Dang it." Al spit. "You've got to be kidding me. Not on my dime!"

CHAPTER THIRTEEN

I nstead of leaving right away, Hank and Jerry stayed. The news of the footage of this hit man running away from the scene made it more urgent for Hank and Jerry to find just who was sending those threatening notes to Judie.

The entire time Al and Tucker had talked to me and with the flurry of activity in front of the motel, I found it interesting the door of room two never opened. Coke had told me it was where Judie and Powell were staying. There was never a better time to go question Judie and get a good look at all the letters.

When she did finally answer the door, a light-blue eye-covering sleeping mask was all discombobulated up on her forehead, shoving the front of her hair upward. Her cheetah-print robe hung loose around her, and the tie was dragging the floor.

"I'm sorry, Judie. Remember I met you at the stalls yesterday? I'm working for Hank Sharp and Jerry Truman on your case."

My words were met with her squinting a few times before it really registered who I was. She nodded, waving me into the dark room.

"I'm sorry. My husband gave me a sleeping pill." She looked out the door. "What's going on out there?"

She turned on some lights inside of the room. I didn't see her husband and listened for any movement in the motel bathroom. It was silent.

"Angus Coo has been found dead in his room. He had left an apparent suicide note saying he had to end his life because without getting the winning bid on the foal, he was fired anyways. But the video footage retrieved by the sheriff's department proves there was a hitman by the name of Shaw Mole. Do you know him?" I asked.

"No." She pulled the mask off of her face and tossed it on the credenza next to the flower vase filled with local wildflowers native to the land, which Coke freshened up daily. "This is very disturbing. I can't believe that about Angus. Do they think it was the same person? Hit man?"

"We don't know. Apparently it looked as though Mr. Coo had been poisoned, but I'm not sure how yet. We are waiting on the initial coroner's report for those findings, but in the meantime, do you know why anyone would want him dead?" I asked.

"No. He was one of the best horse trainers around and acquired a lot of horses over the course of years. But as with everything, younger people come in, and they end up doing better, getting savvier deals." She sighed as though she had a heavy heart.

"Really we believe it was someone Angus knew. There wasn't any forced entry, and if he was poisoned as the coroner believes, then the two glasses next to the table should provide some DNA. Could the person threatening you have any links to the horse auction?"

"My goodness. I would think people love what I've done with the organization. I'm saving lives by having these amazing animals around people who need therapy." She was very offended by my question. "I'm saving lives, not taking them. And if it means picking the best foals around to help someone with PTSD or any sort of health issues by letting them pet or ride a horse, or even muck a horse's stall, then I don't care who wants me dead."

"I'm not so sure it's about the horses. Who else knew you won the lottery?"

The door opened to the room.

"I'm sorry. I didn't know you had company. I thought you might still be sleeping." Powell walked in with a cup of coffee.

"Dear, this is the girl helping the private investigators. Did you see that Angus Coo is now dead?" She dabbed the edges of her eyes with the sleeve of her robe.

"Yes. I was in Evan's room while I let you sleep, and we watched all the police activity. They can't possibly think it has to do with you, do they?" he asked, looking at me for answers.

"They aren't sure. I was telling your wife there is an ID on the shooter. His name is Shaw Mole." Powell looked as confused as his wife. "There's an APB put out by the rangers."

"That's fantastic." Powell went over to his wife's side to comfort her.

"I was just asking Judie who knew she'd won the lottery."

"Of course word got around, since we have gotten so many letters. We don't really know who knows, because we don't talk about it." Powell looked at Judie. "Did you bring the letters?"

"Yes." Judie got up and walked over to the credenza, where she pulled out a drawstring cloth bag. "These are some I'd gotten in the mail as well as found lying at the gate of our home."

"Do you mind if I take them so we can compare?" I wasn't sure if we could compare return addresses or even handwriting, but I knew we wouldn't be able to get prints. I was sure so many people had touched them.

"Take them. We just want you to catch whoever is threatening my wife. As we've seen, they will stop at nothing to follow through." Powell referred to the gun for hire.

"Can I ask you a question about Evan?" I knew it would be a touchy subject. Most parents were when it came to their children.

But I knew better than anyone how rebellious children could be. I had been there myself.

"What about him?" Judie's face jerked up. Her eyes met mine. "He would never hurt me."

"I'm not saying he would. Is there anyone close to him that would want money? Or anyone who knows he is heir to your fortune?" I asked.

"Heir?" She snickered despite the seriousness of our conversation. "No one is getting the winnings. I put them all into the foundation. Everything. Our lives haven't changed. We are still the average people we were before, and that's why it's been so hard to turn people down."

"You aren't taking a dime?" I needed to clarify.

"No. And Evan knows that. He has no problem." She made him sound like he was the perfect son. "He loves me and his father."

"It doesn't mean he's not making a good salary as an employee." Powell made clarification enough for me to talk to Evan.

"So really the lottery money being put into the foundation also pays for people's salaries who work events such as this?"

"Correct. The three of us draw a salary. We pay Iona as well as Delaney. Plus we have to pay for the stalls. The fundraiser is a big part of getting the money so we can continue the upkeep of our horses. So when we need good breeding for the foals to be auctioned off, I'm serious when it comes to the best out there." Judie's passion shone through.

"I've taken up enough of your time." I looked at Powell. "You said you were with your son. Where is he now? We'd like to get his perspective on if he's heard anything that might give us a lead as to who hired Shaw Mole to kill his mother."

Powell looked at his watch.

"He should be down at the stable. He will be making sure the foals sold from yesterday's auction get moved today." Powell rubbed his wife's back.

"If you remember anything," I reiterated, "a conversation, a remark, anything—all information, including tidbits, are extremely important when piecing together why someone would go to the extreme to hire someone to kill."

It was so true that many times it was the little bits of information that filled in the gaps that led me right to a killer.

I took the cloth bag of letters with me and headed straight down to the barn. The sheriff's department was still assessing the Angus Coo crime scene. The hearse was gone from the parking lot, so I knew Colonel Holz had taken Angus's body away.

There was a flurry of activity at the stables. Big trucks with horse trailers hitched to them were lined up, one after the other. Everyone seemed to be busy.

I had no idea what I was looking for or wanting to hear. I did know I wanted to ask Evan about seeing him with the Normal Baptist preacher.

"Ma'am, ma'am!" I heard someone calling for a woman, and when I looked around to see who was screaming, I noticed it was Evan yelling directly at me.

I pointed to myself, and he nodded.

"Ma'am, can you please move out of the way?" He was holding the reins of a foal with one hand and pointing behind me with the other, forcing me to look over my shoulder.

"Oh." I took a few fast steps out of the way of a truck pulling a trailer, almost more offended that Evan had called me "ma'am" than practically getting run over by a truck.

I stood off to the side, watching the truck pull up. Evan, along with Delaney, maneuvered the foal into the trailer. Iona had a clipboard and some paperwork for the driver to sign while the trailer was locked up by Evan. Delaney disappeared into the barn then quickly emerged with another foal as the one truck they'd just loaded drove off.

They did this a couple of times, and when I noticed a lull in the action, I walked over.

"Evan." I introduced myself and decided to take the moment to ask my questions. "We are trying to figure out why someone would want to kill your mom."

"She's powerful," Delaney butted in. "Most people in the horse industry are men. Look around."

Evan laughed.

"Mom can be pretty hard on people." He smirked. "I'm sure since she hired you that you know she won the lottery."

"Yes. And got a lot of letters seeking help or donations." I held the bag up. "I'm taking these back to the office to get analyzed."

Analyzed by me, I left out. But in this case, they didn't need to know that. I mentioned it only to evoke a fear in case they knew I might find out something. In that case, they might let something slip.

"Good. I hope you find out who did this," Iona snarled. Delaney and Evan agreed with her.

"None of you have any idea who it could be?" I asked.

"I would've said Angus Coo, but I found out someone got to him too." Evan had a hard look on his face. "He was pretty mad we didn't let him win the foal."

"What do they think about Ashley?" Delaney asked. "If she wasn't dead, I would've thought she'd be someone to threaten Judie."

"From the looks of the scene and the trajectory of the bullet, it looks like she was an innocent bystander." I hated that so much.

"That's awful." Iona frowned.

"Evan, can I talk to you for a minute?" I asked.

"Sure." He looked at Iona. "What's the time?"

"About fifteen minutes." She looked at the clipboard.

"I have fifteen minutes until the next round of new owners picking up their foals." He walked over toward the dirt ring Coke used for the horse lessons she offered here for locals. She also had a business where anyone could do horseback tours on the trails. "We can talk over here."

I followed him. He bent down, snapped a piece of grass, and stuck it in the corner of his mouth.

"I saw you this morning in a booth at the Caboose Diner with the local preacher."

I noticed his jaw stiffen. He put his boot up on the bottom rung of the fence and hung both arms over the top rung. He didn't look at me. He stared at horses in the ring that weren't their horses, but Coke Ogden's.

"Can you tell me why you'd want to see a preacher?"

"Am I under suspicion of trying to kill my mom?" he asked. "Because I didn't."

"As you know, your mom hired us to find out who is sending these letters. We also know there was a gun-for-hire plot where Ashley Marzullo got killed as well as Angus Coo was poisoned." I leaned on the fence. "I hate to ask you these questions, but no one is off-limits until we can scratch them off. When I saw you with a preacher, one that you don't know or I assume you don't know, it does seem suspicious. Like you're trying to get something off of your chest."

He put his foot on the ground. The piece of grass bobbled from his tongue fiddling with it. He stared at me. I could almost see him processing what he was going to say to me.

"It's none of your business. But I will tell you that I'm not surprised someone tried to kill her. Like I said, she's hard, and she's a shrewd businesswoman. It takes guts to get into the horse industry, much less an organization that wants to use the best of the best for people to pet, groom, and just be around instead of racing them." He spit the piece of grass out. The end of it was all gnawed up and wadded up on the ground. He used his boot to rub it into the dirt.

"I think we are done here. I hope you catch whoever did this." He walked off, and when he wasn't looking, my gag reflexes went off when I picked up the chewed-up piece of grass with his DNA all over it.

CHAPTER FOURTEEN

The Laundry Club Ladies were waiting for me when I got to book club a little late.

"Sorry, y'all." I juggled the box of cookies from the Cookie Crumble that I had barely had time to pick up before Christine Watson closed for the night. "Things have gotten a little crazy since Tucker ID'ed a gun for hire to try to kill Judie Doughty."

"I tell you what." Queenie had on her shiny orange leggings, matching sweatshirt with "Jazzercise" printed across it, and an orange headband pushing her short blond hair off her face. She unzipped her fanny pack and took out her lipstick. She applied a fresh coat.

We all gave her a funny look.

"If I put on lipstick, I won't eat a cookie." She worked so hard to keep her sixty-something figure in shape.

"I'll take hers." Dottie put both her hands in the cookie box and pulled out two big cookies.

"As I was saying," Queenie continued, "not many people in that fundraiser spoke too highly of the Doughtys."

"I heard that, too, but I didn't want to say anything," Betts said. She got up and walked over to the vending machine where customers could buy laundry detergent after a customer was banging on the glass front.

"Did you hear any specifics?" I asked.

"I didn't hear a thing." Abby shook her head. "I was too busy wondering what book we were going to read next. I was hoping we'd pick the next Nadine book." She reached down and grabbed a new Christmas release from her favorite author, who had actually come to our book club after she'd booked a camper in Happy Trails Campground as a winter writing retreat.

"I love me a good Christmas romance and kiss under that mistletoe." Dottie chowed down on another cookie.

"You better take it easy," Queenie warned her. "All those extra calories add up."

"You mind your business." Dottie stuffed the cookie in her mouth.

The more we tried to change Dottie's eating habits, smoking habit, and physical health, the more she pushed back.

"I'm just saying it because I love you, that's all." Queenie moved the conversation to Abby. "You were late the other night, so I bet that's why you didn't hear all the gossip beforehand."

"I got there as soon as the auction was over. Coke handed me a tray of those finger sandwiches and took my bag, sending me right out there." Abby laughed. "I was late because I had this guy at the library looking at all the maps of the trails."

"What?" The whole maps-and-trail thing got my attention.

"I don't know his name. Why?" Abby wondered.

"Did you see what map and trails he was looking at?" I had to know, just in case it was the gun for hire making his escape.

"He mentioned the fundraiser." Abby's eyes grew big. "He said he wasn't staying at the motel but knew there were some good trails to hike. I told him about your new trail. I told him about the cascades at Cat Camp Creek and Tear Trace Trail." She gulped.

"Do you remember what he looks like?" I had to know if this was him. I quickly sent Hank a text asking if he had a photo of Shaw Mole.

"I would probably recognize him." She picked up a cookie, split it in half, and gave me one half. "Let's go over the timeline."

"Thank goodness. I didn't even get the book for book club. I just

71

come to be with y'all and eat." Dottie never read the book, but she was right. It was great to get together. "When I let Fifi and Chester out to potty before I left, I got the notebook out of May-bell-ine's camper just in case."

Dottie pulled the Laundry Club Ladies' clue-gathering notebook from her purse.

"Good thinking!" I was excited to see she'd brought it. She handed it to Abby, and Abby flipped past all the notes and written-down clues we'd gathered over the past few years in different crimes that'd happened in and around the Daniel Boone National Forest.

Abby was the unofficial secretary of the group. Even though it was good to toss ideas around with Hank and Jerry, it was this group that threw out so many good ideas and theories, and did a tad bit of snooping to get clues that led to the killer.

"All right. Mae, start from the beginning." Abby put the pen to paper.

"Jerry and Hank called me in to do a bit of snooping around at the places Judie had frequented to see if she'd mentioned anything to the proprietors or if the proprietors noticed any unusual people hanging around, so we could see if the person sending the notes to Judie was following her. Or if Judie mentioned in passing something that she'd not even considered a clue as to who it might be." I talked, and Abby wrote down the main points.

"We all know that more than likely the person sending the notes is someone she knows." Betts made a very good point.

"Yes. We will list those in a minute," Abby agreed. "Go on, Mae."

"I went to see Coke since she was hosting the event at the Old Train Station, and she hadn't seen anything unusual, nor did Helen Pyle at Cute-icles. But Sally Ann did mention Judie told her about winning the lottery." I continued to talk while Abby wrote "lottery" really big at the top of the piece of paper then circled it a few times. "I thought it was all about the lottery, but the notes I was able to glance through show dates previous to the lottery winning."

I set the bag of notes Judie let me take on the small table in the book club reading corner of the laundromat. Betts had designated areas for different types of activities for her customers to enjoy, so it wasn't just a place to do laundry.

Her thoughts—and they were great—were that if you had to do laundry, you might'swell have some comforts from home. That's how she came up with the couple of couches facing a television corner of the laundromat, the game table area with all the jigsaw puzzles and card games plus many more, then the coffee stand with complimentary coffee which led into the bookshelf area, where we hosted book club once a month.

"This is interesting." Queenie had taken a letter from the bag, as did the rest of the ladies so they could see what type of letters Judie had gotten after she won the lottery.

"As you can see by the photo I took from the investigation office"—I pulled out my phone and showed them the photos I'd taken from Jerry's files—"the dates on the return envelopes from the threats are before the lottery."

"Which means it was probably someone she knew or did business dealings with." Abby and I were both on the same page.

"Yep." I snapped my finger and pointed to her. "We can fast-forward to the day of the attempted hit on her life that took Ashley's and Angus Coo's."

"Angus Coo's?" Dottie leaned back. She took out a cigarette from the case and held on to it. "I thought he overdosed or something."

"Al Hemmer had ruled it a suicide because Angus had left a note, but in reality, there were two glasses." I left out the part where I'd gotten the piece of grass from Evan in hopes I could get it to Agnes so they could run a DNA test on it. Then they could compare the glass and the grass. "He had the gun that killed Ashley, but there was a hit man on video shooting the gun and running off into the woods."

"So that's why you think the person at the library was the killer." Ashley gasped. "Let me know when Hank sends you the photo so I can see if that's him."

"Now that you told me about this guy at the library, I think I'll pay Glenda Russel and Tex a visit now that they are back in the woods." I was talking about one of our good friends, Glenda Russel, and her business partner and possible boyfriend, though we didn't know for sure, Tex the shirtless chiropractor.

Glenda and Tex loved to live in the deep woods in nature. Last winter they had stayed in one of my bungalows when it was too cold to sleep outside, and Glenda started a mobile spa, the Pamper Camper.

Glenda and Tex were so tuned in with the woods around them, they would've seen or heard something or someone. I was one hundred percent positive of that.

"So we can rule out Ashley and Angus, both of whom did have obvious motive to kill Judie." Abby crossed their names off the list. "What about others?"

"Powell, Judie's husband, and Evan, her son." I held up two fingers. "Only for the fact that neither of them get any lottery money because she's funneled all of it back into the Hopes with Horses organization." I held up a finger. "They both get a salary from the organization, and Evan takes over the business."

"He has clear motive if she's not running things the way he likes." Queenie said what I was alluding to.

"And Evan was at the Caboose Diner with the Normal Baptist Church preacher." I tilted my head with my brows lifted. "That tells me he has a guilty conscience about something."

"Andy?" Betts questioned. "Well, we can find out what that's about." She crossed her arms. "He owes me a favor anyways."

"Then we need to go see him." I knew it wouldn't be tonight because I was tired, and the case wasn't going to be solved by running to him this late.

Our little visit to see the preacher would have to wait until tomorrow.

"Now to the real question." Abby smiled. "Tell us the juicy details about you and Hank."

"Huh," Dottie harumphed, crossing one leg over the other. Her foot swung in the air as though she were annoyed. "Someone did come to the campground looking for Hank."

Dottie's comment swept right on past me.

"Don't leave anything out." Betts moved up to the edge of her seat. All eyes were on me.

CHAPTER FIFTEEN

I t looked like fireflies dotted all around the edge of the lake when I pulled back in to Happy Trails Campground after the Laundry Club Ladies and I had gotten a game plan together to look at a few details having to do with Judie Doughty.

My car rolled to a stop, and I realized it wasn't fireflies but lanterns. Hundreds of small lanterns. The darkness already lay along the ground and through the trees, drawing up to the sky with the stars twinkling.

Nightfall came early as the season transitioned to fall, making the temperature perfect for the romantic scene someone had planned for a special loved one.

A flicker of light came from a table set up on the pier on the far side of the lake. I couldn't see everything going on at the pier due to the darkness, but I could see someone sitting in a chair at the table.

I smiled. Whoever did this went to great lengths to make someone very happy. I couldn't wait to ask Dottie who had planned the special event. Since I'd been busy helping Hank and Jerry out, I had let her handle all the requests which needed to be made for such an occasion, as well as all the themed baskets.

I turned off the lights of my car and let it roll down the road so I didn't disturb any of the romantic moments taking place across the lake.

I got out of the car and took one last look before I walked to my campervan.

There was a note taped to the door. I took it off and held it so I could make out what it said by the light of the moon, since we didn't have a whole lot of lights in the campground due to the fact that people came here to get away from the big city lights and be in nature.

Come join me on the pier for a romantic supper. Hank

"Hank?" I questioned and jerked around to see him standing at the edge of the wooden dock with the silhouettes of Chester and Fifi next to him. "Oh my gosh."

My heart melted as it occurred to me that this was for me.

I sucked in a deep breath and smiled, taking the first steps to walk around the lake. Each step I took made my heart beat a little faster, my palms sweat, and my smile grow even bigger than I ever thought possible.

"This is beautiful," I gushed, falling into his arms when he met me on the dry dock side of the pier.

"I hope you're surprised." He held me tight, stroking my hair. "I knew I needed to make up to you how I just left and didn't let you know. It was something I had to do. Go. Be by myself in the woods and just stay there with my head down while I did a couple of cases. Just me and Chester figuring out what I wanted to do when I grow up." I felt him laugh before his chest let out a long breath. "I woke up and realized it was here. Right here. With you."

"You have no idea how happy that makes me." I pulled back slightly and kissed him. "I can't believe Dottie let you do this."

We stood next to each other, holding hands, looking around.

"It took a lot of convincing to even get her to listen to me. She slammed the office door in my face, then I waited and followed her to her camper, where she kept trying to jab me with her cigarette while telling me she was going to burn me." He shook his head. "I think she sees you as her daughter, not her employer or friend."

"Honestly, she was a rock for me when you left. I knew we were on a different path for that season and trying to figure out who and what we would become as we entered into our thirties, but the hurt was still there." I wrapped my arms around his one arm and rested my head on his shoulder.

"Over the past couple of days, I realized how careful you are when it comes to figuring out clues for these crimes. I let my heart take over my head, and it was an ego thing for me to be upset when you got involved in cases, only because I couldn't imagine what people would say if you got hurt—or worse killed—and even her own boyfriend couldn't save her." It was reassuring to hear him realize he was the one getting in our way. "I talked to Bobby Ray, and he said that you've always been that way. The first time I met you was on this very pier. You were just as hardheaded then, and I was instantly attracted to how strong and inde-pendent you are."

"And that's what I loved about you." I didn't tell him how that was the main reason I couldn't date Ty Randal, though Ty and I had tried it out. "I love how you challenged me to be the best and not just take whatever came my way."

"And I also love how you defend your friends and your loyalty to them." Hank was right about that. "The slightest bit of criticism of them, and you're on it." He peeled my hands off his arm and wrapped it around me. "You are loyal to me."

"Yes, I am." I looked up at him.

"I am going to prove just how loyal I'm going to be to you. This is just one of many romantic nights for the rest of our life." He hugged me to him.

The rest of our lives sounded like a good plan to me.

CHAPTER SIXTEEN

R *uff, ruff.* Fifi, my alarm, sounded way too early the next day.
"The alarm hasn't even gone off." I rolled over and looked at
the clock. "We have ten minutes."

Grrrr, ruff! Her growl and bark got louder.

"Fine." I swung my legs over the bed, reached over, and tapped the
alarm off. "I'm coming! Geez, hold your horses," I told Fifi, who was
now scratching at the door.

I took my sweatshirt off the back of the chair on my way out of my
bedroom and pulled it over my head, knowing it was going to be a brisk
morning walk with her. My coffeepot alarm had already gone off. I
sucked in a deep breath of the fresh aroma and woke up my mind
enough to recall just how special Hank had made last night.

I unlocked the camper door, and Fifi darted out, greeting a wagging-
tailed Chester.

"Good morning." Hank was sitting at my picnic table with two mugs
and a carafe of coffee. "Chester has been waiting for her to come out."

"And you?" I walked over and bent down to kiss him.

"I've been waiting for you to let her out." He picked up the carafe
and poured two cups of coffee. "I wanted to watch the sunrise with
you."

"Come on then." I took the mug and walked across the road to the shores of the lake.

I had placed several Adirondack chairs around so campers could just stop and take a seat to enjoy all parts of the campground. It was perfect to sit, have a cup of coffee, and watch the sun pop over the tips of the trees or even watch the sun dip down at dusk.

"I told Jerry I would finish up some of the background checks for some of the folks who were on the guest list. So far nothing has turned up that would even associate Shaw Mole to the hire." Hank looked stumped. He set his mug on the arm of the chair. "This is really crazy. The two people who would have motive to kill Judie or even send threatening letters to her are dead."

"And from the evidence it doesn't appear to be driven by the lottery money." It was apparent. "I am going to go back to the motel and go see Glenda. From what I understand, if the person from the library I told you about last night was Shaw Mole and was looking for trails and how to escape easily, I know Glenda or Tex had to have seen him, or maybe they've heard something."

"Good idea," he agreed.

"Plus I want to go with Betts to see the preacher." I reminded him how Betts cleaned the church today, so it would be a good time to go help her late this morning after I left the motel.

"Well, you let me know as soon as you hear anything." He and I made a plan to get together later that afternoon since it was my turn to work the campground. "I thought maybe me and you could go out to supper with Abby and Bobby Ray."

"I would love that." It was so nice to have Hank back, even though I still wasn't used to the beard. I'd never tell him, but I really wished he'd shave it. "Thank you for last night if I forgot to thank you."

"You didn't. But you better buckle up, because there's going to be a lot more where that came from." He leaned over and gave me a proper good-morning kiss before we parted ways.

After I got dressed for the day, fed Fifi, and texted Dottie about letting Fifi out until I got back for my office shift, I remembered to get the baggie filled with the grass clipping from Evan. I wanted to take that along with the leftover cookies to the Normal sheriff's department to give to Agnes.

I'd forgotten to tell Hank about my thoughts, but it could wait until later this afternoon. With Fifi all set and Dottie on the hook to come down and get her, I was off and running with full intentions of discovering new details that would lead to clues to who wanted Judie Doughty dead.

The trails around the motel property were considered to be pretty intense. That's why I had used my job on the National Park Committee to find trails that weren't as difficult so people with small children or elderly parents, or even just anyone who liked to hike on an even, level trail, could visit the amazing cascades in the deep wooded area behind the Old Train Station Motel.

I'd even used Mary Elizabeth as a guinea pig. But in Mary Elizabeth style, she wore the most ridiculous outfit to hike in as well as shoes. When she tripped, fell, and hurt her back, we were lucky Glenda Russel had taken on the hippie life and was living in the woods with Tex, the shirtless chiropractor, who literally fixed Mary Elizabeth right on up.

That's how we knew Glenda was back in town after she'd left, but I knew she'd eventually turn up because Rosa, her horse, was a resident at the stables at the Old Train Station barn. Glenda had even agreed to let Rosa be a trail horse for Coke's tourist trail rides.

Glenda Russel was exactly where I thought she'd be on this cool, early-fall morning.

"I thought I'd find you here." I looked into Rosa's stall, where Glenda was brushing her.

"Good morning. To what do I owe the surprise visit?" Glenda patted Rosa on the butt and tossed the horse brush into the bucket before she came over and slid the stall door wide open. "I would give you a big hug, but I'm dirty from her. She's not been brushed since the fundraiser, then Al Hemmer wouldn't let me in until they cleared the scene."

"They cleared the scene?" I questioned.

"Yeah. Last night. He called around eight p.m. and said I might get a call from someone from the FBI since the case involves some guy on the FBI's most wanted," she said. "Anyways, I'm just glad my girl is okay. Oh, is Mary Elizabeth okay?"

"Oh, yeah. She's fine. I'm here probably for the same reason the FBI might get in contact with you." I briefly told her about how I was helping Jerry and Hank with the case.

"I heard Hank was back. No wonder you're glowing." She pinched her lips and shook her head. "You two are meant to be. But you're not here to talk about him." She winked. "Here." She walked over and took two horse brushes out of the bucket and tossed me one. "Get to brushing, and we can chat."

"I've never brushed a horse before." Rosa was a bit intimidating to me.

"Don't let her know that." Glenda gave me a quick tutorial on brushing, and my phone chirped a text.

I took it out of my pocket and looked at the photo Hank had texted of Shaw Mole.

"See, her tail is swishing. She likes you." Glenda had gone from brushing to picking Rosa's hooves.

"Hank texted me a photo of the hit man they are looking for because he's the one seen running from the barn." I showed Glenda the phone. She put down the hoof, and we stepped out of the stall and into the barn light. "I haven't confirmed with Abby, but I think he was in the library right before the fireworks because Abby had someone in there asking about the trails around the Old Train Station Motel. Abby was late to helping Coke out for the party after the auction, which would give her time to get here and the hit man time to get here."

"I saw him." She poked my phone screen. "In fact, Tex and I were at the cascades the night of the shooting. We went down there to watch the fireworks and have a romantic night. That guy right there was running down the trail and ruined the moment for us. He was startled when he saw me and Tex. He said he was lost and asked for directions."

"Did he have a gun?" This was a major question because we knew

Angus Coo skipped the party, and the gun was found in his motel room.

"No. Nothing." She continued to look at the photo. "Tex said he found it odd that someone would be on the trails that late and without any gear. Very suspicious."

"This explains a lot." I was beginning to wonder if Angus Coo had hired the hit man, and when the deal went south after Shaw Mole accidentally killed Ashley, he killed Angus so nothing could be traced back to him.

Things were taking a huge turn, and I needed to pick Agnes Swift's brain.

I thanked Glenda for her time and told her she should probably let Al Hemmer know they'd seen the hit man identified as Shaw Mole.

On my way out of the barn, I glanced over at the riding ring at the other barn Coke had let Judie use for the foals. Tucker Pyle was standing there talking to Delaney Harrison. That didn't seem unusual to me. He was probably getting her last statement before she left town.

I hung around a minute or two, trying to decide if I should tell Tucker to go in and see Glenda, but I didn't want to put that pressure on Glenda.

At this point, it was a good possibility Angus had hired Shaw to be put on standby to kill Judie. And by standby, I meant that Shaw was there to make the hit if things didn't go well for Angus, and boy, things hadn't gone well.

Then on the flip side, maybe Evan had a laid-out plan. I was glad I stayed hidden next to the barn, because when Tucker left, Evan emerged when he must've thought it was safe. It was then I watched Delaney Harrison and Evan break out into what appeared to be a heated argument right before she smacked him right across the face.

With that little bit of information tucked into my brain, I slipped back across the field unnoticed and drove back toward town, stopping in the business district where the places like the doctors' offices, bank, Cookie Crumble, and the courthouse were located.

Even though there'd been a lot of talk and promises from the mayor of Normal—she'd vowed to move the sheriff's department out of the back of the courthouse so they could expand the courthouse—it'd yet been done.

I pulled up to the back, where the sheriff's department was located, and walked into the entrance, where there was a small window where dispatcher Agnes Swift sat. She had to buzz you through the other door to let you in.

"Ding, ding," I called into the open sliding window and looked at the nameplate that had Agnes's name engraved on it. "I've brought your favorite cookies," I called out.

"It's 'bout time you get down here and see me." Agnes came out of the bathroom, drying her hands on a paper towel. "When is my grandson coming? I heard he was back in town."

"He's not stopped by?" I questioned, finding that very odd since he told me he was going to check with her on the footage, and now he'd sent me the photo.

"No, and I'm going to whoop his butt." She wagged a finger before she took that finger and hit the button to buzz me into the department. Her gray hair curls were really tight to her head. This was a sign she'd gone down to Cute-icles to get her weekly dose of gossip and hair fix from Helen.

"Where is everyone?" I questioned when I noticed she was alone and during a morning of a very important investigation.

"Al had to call in the FBI. He's on the phone with them and the other deputies in the interrogation room." She shook her head and took the bag of cookies. "I was hoping Hank would come back to work, but I've not heard anything about it. Though I did hear some rumblings about you and Hank." She took a bite of the cookie and smiled. Her saggy jowls swayed as she chewed. "I'm sure that's why he's not been here to see me. He's busy making up with you. And by all rights, that's fine by me. That boy messed up."

So she didn't know Hank was working for Jerry at the investigation office? Helen hadn't told her?

"Did you know Jerry was working on the Judie Doughty case?" I asked.

"I was looking through that file and noticed he had given Al his file on the case, but now that there's two dead, I didn't think Jerry was doing any investigating."

The bell dinged at the window, and we looked over. There was a man in a ranger's hat standing there, looking at us.

"Can I help ye?" Agnes walked over to see what he wanted. "No. He doesn't work here. He went to Mammoth Cave District to work."

There were a few words exchanged.

"Yes. I'm his granny, so when you find him, you tell him I've got a bone to pick with him." She and the man said their goodbyes after a few mumbles.

"What was that about?" I asked.

"Not sure, but when you get done playing kissy face with my grandson, you tell him to come see me." Agnes was pretty good about keeping secrets, and from what I just witnessed, someone was asking her about Hank.

Didn't Dottie mention someone had come to the campground office asking about him too? I put the question in my memory to ask Dottie about it.

"I will, but right now I wanted to talk to you about the Judie Doughty case. I told Judie I would continue to look into it, and I can't help but think it's her son Evan." I pulled the baggie out of my bag.

"I wouldn't doubt it." Agnes had seen so much during her time in the sheriff's office that nothing seemed to faze her. "It's generally someone close to the victim."

"There's been some sketchy activity with the son. For one, he isn't going to get any of the lottery winnings because Judie put it into the Help for Horses Foundation. But he is on salary. Then I saw him having an argument with Delaney Harrison, the main horse trainer for Judie. She even slapped him. When I saw the two glasses in Angus Coo's motel room, I knew Angus had someone there. I'm not sure, and the timeline really doesn't add up for Evan to have been with Angus during the fireworks or after, since I'd seen him by Judie's side the entire time, but it could've been from earlier in the day. So I picked this up after Evan chewed on it and was hoping to compare the DNA on this to the DNA Al will get back from the glasses." I jiggled the baggie in the air.

"I can't guarantee anything, but I'll try my hardest," Agnes said. My phone chirped. "My grandson?" Her gray brows dipped.

"No. Mary Elizabeth, and she wants to host a cookout for Hank being back in town tomorrow night. So can you and Precious come? I'd love to see my grand-puppy." I made Agnes giggle every time I referred to Precious as my grand-puppy since she was one of Fifi's puppies she'd had with Rosco.

"I'm not gonna turn down seeing you or my grandson." She went back to answering the dispatch phone.

Unfortunately, I left the department with more questions than I had before, only they were about Hank and why he hadn't gone to see his granny.

CHAPTER SEVENTEEN

M any times on my way over to meet Betts at the Normal Baptist
Church, I hit the button on the Focus steering wheel to tell the
voice on command to call Hank, but didn't.

It was one of those things that I questioned about the relationship
Hank and I had. He was trusting me with helping out and keeping
myself safe, and I had to trust there was nothing going on with him and
believe he'd just been so busy since he'd gotten in town that he'd not
been able to see Agnes or even get the information he wanted from her.

Things came up, and I sure did understand that.

"What's going on with you?" Betts was already waiting for me in the
parking lot of the church. She handed me a cleaning bucket, which was
my cover to get inside. "You look preoccupied."

"I'm sure it's nothing." I took the bucket to follow her up the
concrete steps of the church. Normal Baptist Church was actually a
pretty big church and the second-largest building in Normal, the courthouse being the first.

The twenty pillars, ten on each side, on the outside framed the
entrance.

Betts pulled the door open and held it with her foot for me to go
ahead.

"Do you think it's odd Hank hasn't seen Agnes?" I asked and waited inside of the vestibule.

"It's odd, but do you think he's been wanting to make sure you two are good before he goes to see her, where you know she's going to question him up and down?" She flipped on the lights, bringing to life the stained-glass windows that illustrated old Bible stories in color.

We walked down the rows of pews and up to the altar, where I waited for Betts to say a prayer before she got started spraying furniture polish all over the church pews.

"Possibly," I finally answered her after I'd waited for her to do her ritual of praying before she started her cleaning process. I'd helped her so much before that I knew how she did things. "I guess so." I decided to take what she said and agree to it since it was the most logical thing.

Or maybe he was not ready to go back into the department since he did quit. I didn't know. I just knew it was strange, and I would be sure to ask him later.

"I thought I saw the van out front." The interim preacher, Andy, stood in the back of the church. His voice echoed. "How are you, Betts?"

"I'm good. Glad to see so many new faces on the tithe list this week." Betts was still so involved in church, even after Lester had gone to prison.

Lester Hager was the last full-time preacher at the church and Betts's ex-husband, who she still went to see at the local prison during the Bible Thumpers' prison ministry. I was in no way going to judge her for what she was doing. I didn't understand, but it was her tale to tell me if she wanted me to know.

I hid my smile as I went down the pews with a clean rag, wiping off the polish while Betts talked to him.

"Yes. Enrollment has been up. I like that." He smiled and looked at me. "I'm hoping to get the full-time position here, and I heard the board is going to be voting on it during this month's meeting."

"Yes. I do believe I noticed it was on the docket, along with so many other things, like next year's budget." Betts had a funny way of dealing with church people. Though she didn't say it, she told him in so many words, in her nice way, that they would be discussing the salary needed to keep him, and if it fit in the budget, then he could possibly be getting the job.

"Let's all pray it works out. I think it would be great to bring up a family here." He glanced over at me. "Hello, Mae."

Betts picked up the duster. She batted it around the hymnals in the pew pockets.

"Hi." I was taken aback a little on how he knew me. "How did you know my name?" I was curious.

"I think everyone in town knows you since you've done so much for the community, but Mary Elizabeth loves to carry a photo of you in her Bible." He let the cat out of the bag. "She pulls it out at the end of Sunday school every week, and when it's time for prayer requests, you're always her pick."

"Oh." My lips formed an O as the embarrassment crept up my face.

"I tell her that even though she wants you in the front pew with her every week, that it doesn't mean you aren't a believer. Everyone has their own special relationship with God, and he's not just located in churches." He made me like the way he thought. "But I'd love to see you here."

"You never know now, do you?" I smiled and took the chance. "Since God loves everyone and everyone has their own special relationship"—I used his own words—"can you tell me what you and Evan Doughty were talking about at the Caboose Diner? I just so happened to see you there. In fact, I've been hired by his mother to find out who is behind the threatening letters she's been receiving. Did he mention anything like that?"

"What I talk to people about is pretty much private unless there's a warrant." His smile faded into a thin line. "It's good seeing you ladies. It always smells so good in here after you clean."

"Thank you." Betts waved the duster in the air.

"Have you gone to see Lester lately?" he asked. I noticed her stiffen. "I was curious what he thought about the article they did on him at the Baptist convention. Did you give it to him?"

"I did. He's good. He liked the article and is excited for the outcome. It was good seeing you." Betts cut off any more conversation with Andy and moved along to dusting the statues a little farther away from where I was cleaning off the polish on the pews.

Preacher Andy left, and when I turned back around to ask Betts about the article Andy had mentioned, she'd disappeared into another part of the church.

This day was shaping up much differently than I'd anticipated. I'd woken up with the idea of having my questions answered, not piling more on.

I was there helping Betts as a coverup to getting some answers from Preacher Andy, but I wasn't going to keep asking him since he definitely stood by his convictions. So after I finished cleaning the pews Betts had put the polish on, I left the rag there and decided to head back to the campground.

There was just enough time for me to check in with Dottie to see if I needed to address anything for the campground or our guests before I took over for the afternoon.

The second shift was actually my favorite to work. I didn't mind the first shift of the day since I was a morning person, but it was the second half of the day, where the guests would be getting back from their adventures, that made the campground come alive.

I loved hearing stories about what they'd discovered in and around the Daniel Boone National Park. The excitement in their eyes when they talked about the gorgeous landscape of our little Kentucky treasure as well as the laughter on their faces as they talked just made everything with the world seem okay.

When I pulled into the campground, I decided to go ahead and park the car at the camper and just walk up. It was turning out to be a much cooler day than average, and some of the guests had their campfires already lit while they chatted with other guests.

I loved this about the campground. Strangers coming together over a campfire, discussing things they've learned about camping, places they've visited, and suggestions for food to try. It was a community of caring individuals that made it so special and unique.

No matter how much money you had, when it came to camping, everyone who was here had that in common, putting any other differences they might have aside.

"Dottie." I let out a loud, open-mouthed sigh when I noticed she'd left the campervan door open. She usually came in and out when she was looking after Fifi. "At least the screen door is shut."

It was the time of year those gross stink bugs liked to get into the campers and just hang out. They didn't do any harm, but they were just nasty and were literally everywhere.

The camper lights were on when I took the one step to get inside.

"Hello?" I reached for a knife from the butcher block knife set on the counter when I noticed a man was sitting with his back to me at the café table. "Can I help you?"

I stood at the door, waiting to either jab him with a knife or take off running, but he didn't move.

"I said, can I help you?" I took a step forward with my arm up in the air, holding the knife above my head so I could be ready to shank him as I tapped him on the shoulder with my other hand.

Slowly the person leaned forward, falling on the table with a thud.

CHAPTER EIGHTEEN

"You're telling me you didn't order any sort of cake from the Cookie Crumble?" Al Hemmer had me sitting outside of my camper at my picnic table. Hank was next to me, Dottie was pacing up and down the road, and Tucker was inside with the dead man, who had a gun and was facedown in a fancy cake that I didn't order.

"No." I gnawed on my lip. "I didn't order any cake. I did pick up some cookies from Christine yesterday for the Laundry Club Ladies' monthly book club. That's it. No cake."

"There's a box in your trash with the cake sitting on the table. Well, it looks like the victim had a piece." Al didn't seem to believe me. "And you didn't invite someone into your camper to have cake?"

"No." I shook my head. "How many times do I need to tell you that I was at the Normal Baptist Church cleaning with Betts? I parked my car, went inside to get ready for my office shift, and walked in to that guy."

I went through the entire turn of events, including the knife thing.

"I can tell you who that is in there." Hank had been the first person I'd called and had seen the man.

Really, I should've called 911, but whenever I was around a dead person, Hank was the one who I called first.

"That's Shaw Mole, the gun for hire to kill Judie Doughty." Hank's words fell on Al.

Al's face stilled. His eyes narrowed, and his lips pursed. His cheeks slightly drew in as he pondered what Hank had said.

"Yep." Al tugged on the waist of his sheriff's uniform pants. He inhaled a big sniff through his nose. "I knew that. 'Scuse me." He headed back into my camper.

"He's something else." Hank looked at me. "You okay?"

"I guess." I gulped and greeted Tucker Pyle when he walked up to us.

"How are you doing?" Tucker asked.

"I was just telling Hank how I keep thinking Shaw Mole was here to finish me off. Did you see the gun in his hand?" After I'd tapped him on the shoulder and he fell forward into the cake, his hand dropped to his side with his finger hooked around a gun with a silencer on the end. "Which means whoever killed Ashley and Angus is still out there." I sighed. "Do you think Shaw had a heart attack?"

"I guess we won't know until Colonel Holz comes and takes a preliminary before they cart the body off." Hank ran his hand along his big beard.

"So you think he was going to bring me a cake to get on my sweet side before he killed me?" I wasn't sure where the cake had come in.

"I do think he was here to get rid of you. I'm not sure where the cake comes in." Tucker sat down on the opposite side of the picnic table, folded his hands, and rested them on the tabletop. "I do know that for him to come here means you've gotten too close to whoever did hire him. Let's think about your activities the past couple of days."

"I don't know, man." Hank put a hand between me and Tucker. "Mae is pretty shaken up about finding that guy in her house. Maybe we should give her a day or even just a few hours to process it."

"No." I shook my head. "I'm good. I think the quicker we get these ideas out of my head and the possibilities of who and why someone has hired this guy, then the faster we can get on with our lives."

"Only if you're sure." Hank had changed from being the final "no" or advising me not to do something to really making sure I was fine.

"Positive," I told both of them.

"Then I'll get with Jerry at the office. You two figure out what our next move will be, and I'll go over to the Old Train Station to let Judie know this guy is dead." Hank got up and kissed me on my head. "Are you sure you're okay?"

"I'm fine. You go, and let's get this taken care of while I go over every move I've made with Tucker." It seemed like the best thing to do. I gave him a reassuring smile to make him feel somewhat better about leaving me there.

Colonel Holz pulled up in his hearse and left a sick feeling deep in my stomach. I was worried the campers would be asking all sorts of questions, and it didn't look too good to have the dead body of a hit man there.

Hank and Colonel talked a few minutes before Hank gave me one last wave. I watched him walk down to his camper and get Chester before they got into his truck and drove out of the campground to go meet Jerry.

"Mae, honey, you've having the worst time." Colonel tsked. "But we'll get him out of your house in no time."

"Thank you." I stood up to greet him like Mary Elizabeth always taught me to do when someone enters the room. Even at my age, my manners she'd made sure I had never went out of style. "Please let me know if you think it was a heart attack or something."

"I will." He headed inside of the camper with his little doctor's bag in his hand.

"What do you say we go over your actions over the last few days? Maybe we can narrow down who else was at the same places you were." Tucker pulled out his little notebook. "I hate that Al called the FBI. It's one of those cases where these killings are happening in my district and his district, but I'd like to get some solid leads for them."

"Outside of the places you knew I went the day of the murders, I went back to the motel to see if Glenda knew anything. I saw Evan Doughty at the barn, and he had an argument with Delaney Harrison. I saw her smack him. And I also saw Evan at the Caboose Diner, having lunch with Andy, the preacher." I could see Tucker doing what I had done about talking to Preacher Andy. "I already went to the church to talk to Andy. He claims he can't talk about it because it's confidentiality between a preacher and a person."

I knew I didn't have the right words, but Tucker knew what I meant.

"I'll go see him." Tucker wrote something down in the notebook. "I'm sure Al can get a warrant or pull some weight around to get Andy to talk."

"If it's any help, Al's family, the Hemmers, tithe a great deal to the church." I only knew this because years ago I'd helped Lester and Betts out with the church's finances and I had access to what people tithe.

It was crazy amounts of money from the Hemmers, and they used it as leverage to get things in town they wanted. Hence, Al Hemmer getting appointed to sheriff when he wasn't nearly qualified.

"Since Gab Hemmer is the president of the National Park Board, I suggest you start with him. You're the ranger. You share the same office building, and I think you can squeeze him." Gab Hemmer didn't like to be pushed around. He liked getting his way, and he certainly liked throwing his weight around.

Tucker Pyle was actually the one in charge if it was all boiled down, which gave Tucker the upper hand. If Tucker really wanted the information about Evan and what he told Preacher Andy, Gab would be the squeeze to get the juice.

"I'll do that." Tucker made another note. "Who else did you see besides Evan?"

"Really no one that I feel like would be part of this. I went to see Agnes Swift." I hadn't told Tucker about my little grass DNA thing, but if I did, he might just be able to get that pushed through too. "Did you process the glasses at Angus Coo's motel room?"

"One of the sheriff's deputies did. Why?" he asked.

"Queenie." I stopped talking. "Listen, I've got to go see Queenie. I'll call you." I got up. "Can you go and get my car keys from inside? I think I dropped them when Shaw Mole fell into the cake."

The cake.

I needed to go see Christine Watson and ask about who sent me a cake. I also needed to go see Queenie because she said she ran into Angus when he ran to his room. Did she see Shaw Mole? Glenda Russel had talked to Shaw, so we knew he ran off, but did he stop and see Angus? Angus was poisoned. Did the same person poison Angus? Did we have two killers?

Tucker got up from the picnic table and passed Colonel Holz on his way inside.

"Did you notice the victim had eaten some of your cake?" Colonel asked.

"Yes. I guess he got tired of waiting on me." I shrugged and then realized it was too simple. "What are you saying?"

"I'm saying he didn't die from a heart attack." Colonel didn't tell me what I wanted to hear. "I looked at the photo Hank had of the victim, and he's definitely taken on a cherry-colored skin color with some changing dark places around his mouth, which tells me he's been poisoned by cyanide. Where did you get the cake?"

"I don't know. My door was open, and when I walked in, I found Shaw Mole and the cake. I didn't buy the cake. I thought maybe he brought it." I looked off into the distance and noticed a different type of ranger vehicle stopped up at the office.

Dottie was up there, so she'd talk to whoever it was getting out. I pushed it out of my head.

"I think someone poisoned the cake and dropped it off for you to eat." He handed me a note. "I found this wadded up on the floor. I'm sure if we took it in for fingerprinting, Shaw Mole's prints would be all over it, because I think he was waiting for you and he couldn't resist a piece of cake."

Colonel showed me a search he'd done on his phone internet.

"This is the gun for hire. His mom is a baker. He used to work in the bakery. I think his sweet tooth got to him. Someone else put the cake there, and he didn't realize it was laced." Colonel Holz's theory was just mind-blowing.

"Are you telling me that not only has someone tried to poison me with cake, but someone else has sent the sharpshooter to kill me?" I was beginning to get a complex.

"Or they wanted to make sure the deed was done." Colonel's head tilted. "I'm not going to know for sure until I get him to the morgue, but from what I can tell from his body, he ate the cake, and now he's dead."

Out of the corner of my eye, I saw Dottie up at the office, staring down at the campground, waving to get my attention.

The ranger car must've driven off when I wasn't looking because it wasn't parked there anymore.

"I'll keep you posted, but watch out." Colonel headed over to his hearse, where he unlatched the back and began the process of taking his gurney out to extract the dead body from my camper.

Though I knew I had two people to go see immediately, I couldn't neglect the campground. If I'd just tell Hank and Jerry they were on their own now that my life had been put in danger, I'd just stick to working here.

One problem.

There was no way I was going to sit around and not try to find out who was out there deliberately trying to kill me.

It was personal now.

CHAPTER NINETEEN

"I'm beginning to think there's a problem." Dottie's cigarette bounced up and down in the corner of her mouth while she nervously picked at her hangnails.

"We do have a problem. Someone wants me dead." I opened the door of the office to let Fifi run out so she could go potty before I went to the Cookie Crumble and the Normal Library to see Abby.

"No. I mean a Hank kinda problem." She took a drag of the cigarette and blew out a long, steady stream of smoke. "I think he's in some sort of trouble."

"What?" I questioned with a laughing undertone, trying not to honestly believe it—only I, too, had wondered when I asked Agnes Swift about him.

"This guy has been here twice looking for Hank. Each time I tell him I ain't seen him since he left for the post in Mammoth Cave because of you. I lied because of you." She pointed her fingers at me with the cig nestled in between them. "That boy is in some trouble. This fish stinks from the head down." She referred to all the goings-on with Hank. "Look at his face. Why's he coverin' up that handsome jawline? Why does he have a new camper when the one he had was much better looking and just fine?"

"Did he say what he wanted with Hank?" There was a bad feeling churning inside of me.

"I didn't ask. I just said I'd give you his card when I saw you." Dottie had covered up for me and Hank. She reached into her shirt. Her fingers fiddled around in her bra until she brought them back out with the card. "Here you go."

I took it by the edge.

"Thanks," I groaned and wished she'd not stuck it in her bra. But oh well. It was Dottie, and she was just not going to change. Nor would I want her to.

"So what are you going to do?" she asked.

Fifi scratched on the office door to be let inside. I opened the door, and she rushed in.

"I'm not sure, but I am going to see Abby at the library. Maybe I'll look this guy up before I call him." I slipped the card in my pocket. "Do you know where Queenie is?"

"She's got a Jazzercise class at the church." Dottie shook her head. "I reckon she thinks I'm gonna get in shape and stop smokin', because every week she sends me that darn exercise schedule." She shook her finger at me. "She's got 'nuther thing comin' to her. I ain't gonna do no Jazzercise."

"Thanks for covering for Hank. I know it's hard for you to trust him back in my life." Dottie held grudges when it came to people who hurt the ones she loved. "For some reason, I really do think he's changed since he left law enforcement. But you're right." It just hurt to think I was about to say what I was going to tell her. "I do think something is going on. He's not gone to see Agnes, and all the things you pointed out, like the beard and the camper, are weird because he's not said a word to me about it."

I stopped. My jaw dropped.

"When I let Chester out, I saw papers scattered all over the floor. I went inside and picked them up. I noticed it was a case from his post at Mammoth Cave. I just thought maybe he forgot to turn in his files." I gulped. "Do you think it has to do with that?"

"It's worth a shot." Dottie flung her finger toward Hank's camper. "You better go get you some photos before you go to the library and look up that case. I'll stay here and work. I ain't got nothin' else to do besides stare down at your camper. I'll keep Fifi."

"And I'm going to get some clothes for Jazzercise." I put my hands together in prayer position. "Thanks, Dottie."

It was lazy for me to jump back in my car to go to Hank's to snoop, and it was just bad that I was going to snoop. I needed to get over to the Cookie Crumble, the library, and the church to follow the leads on who was trying to kill me, but I loved Hank so much that I had to know if he was in danger.

I'd convinced myself there was enough time for me to do it all and just started to check one thing off the ever-growing list.

Just as usual, Hank's door was open. The file had been moved from where I'd put it. After opening a few of his kitchen drawers, I quickly found the file.

I'd seen enough of these files to know what I was looking for. The case was about a man who'd gone missing from the area. Hank was the ranger on duty.

I took a photo of the documents with the man's name and put the file back where I'd found it.

I should've called Hank to ask him about it and tell him a man was looking for him, but why would I burden him while he was on the Judie Doughty case? Hank had seemed much happier working with Jerry than I'd seen him in a long time.

It was nice to have this Hank rather than the stressed-out Hank. This Hank was also better for our relationship. And I was just about to go to any length to make sure this Hank stayed. So if that meant I had to find out who this guy was, then I was going to do it.

When I got back into my car, I took the card out of my pocket and sat there staring at it.

I wondered if I could just give him a call and see what he wanted, or if I should find out about this case Hank had been working on while at the Mammoth Cave post, just to be armed with some knowledge.

Maybe the ranger wasn't here for that case. Then again, I'd never know why he was here and what he wanted with me until I did return his call.

I typed in his phone number and with a trembling hand held the phone up to my ear, trying to prepare myself for what I was about to discover.

Was Hank going to great lengths not to be seen as himself? What disturbed me most was the fact he'd not gone to see his granny.

There was a twinge of relief when the man's answering machine picked up.

"This is John Buxley, the Regional Ranger for the..." He rattled off his title. "Please leave a message, and I or one of my rangers will get back with you."

"Hi, there." I lost my confidence. "This is Sandy Gillery with the Tribune," I said, making up a name and a newspaper. "I'm writing an article on the case of the disappearance of Walter Adams, and I'd like to get a statement from you. Please call me back." Then I said my phone number.

As soon as I hung up, I clicked around my phone to the outgoing messages and deleted the one I'd recorded, replacing it with the phone's auto-generated generic one just in case he called.

There was something to be said about the last few years where I'd found myself putting on my sleuthing hat. I'd like to think I'd gotten a lot smarter.

I pulled around the campground, and when I got to the opposite side of the lake from my camper, I glanced over. Colonel Holz and Al Hemmer were carrying the church cart out of my camper.

Chills ran up my spine.

I gripped the wheel and put John Buxley out of my head. It was time to check the next thing off my list, and that was to go see Christine Watson at the Cookie Crumble.

CHAPTER TWENTY

There was a line out of the door of the Cookie Crumble. From the looks of the packed shop and the full parking lot, Christine Watson's worry and stress about the location of the shop was for nothing.

When Christine and her sister had opened the bakery, there wasn't any open retail space in the downtown area of Normal. There was an old restaurant that'd been closed down for years in the business district. Since it had a kitchen and a large front dining area, it was easy for them to convert the old building into a bakery, and they thought they'd make it temporary until there was a retail space downtown.

Christine had more than enough customers from the businesses in the business district that any of the tourists stopping by was a bonus.

From the license plates and all the camping gear packed in and on top of the cars in the lot, she had her fair share of tourists as well.

"If you love caramel, you're going to love this one." When I went inside, I overheard Christine talking to a customer. "A little crisp on the outside and a bit gooey on the inside."

I had no idea how she did it, but she made the perfect cookie each time.

Christine Watson waved at me from behind the bakery's counter.

The freckles on her face scrunched together on her plump cheeks as her eyes squinted from the smile on her face. Her brown hair was pulled back in its usual ponytail.

I waited patiently and let a few people go ahead of me that'd come in after me because I wanted to talk to her about the cake.

It'd taken about twenty minutes until there was enough time for me to talk to her without a lot of ears around. She was more than happy to give me any information after I told her I thought someone had tried to poison me.

"It was a special-order cake. It was odd. They said they wanted to take it to you themselves on the online form. They even asked if I'd leave it sitting outside after hours." Her telling me it was an online order spoke volumes about the length someone went to in order to make sure they weren't seen or heard. "I tried to call the phone number from the form, but it was bogus."

"They would have to pay with a credit card online, right?" I asked.

"Yes. I can get that number for you if you'd like. In this circumstance, I don't believe they have any right to stop me from giving out their information, as long as you don't use it." She said something to one of her employees and had me follow her back into the bakery office, where I took a seat while she clicked away on the computer. "Yes. It's right here."

"Can you print out the order? The directions and everything?" I asked.

"I sure can." With the click of her keyboard, the printer sitting on the corner of her desk buzzed and spit out the details of the order. "The credit card is blurred there, but I can pull it up on our account."

"Perfect." I took the piece of paper off the printer. She continued to get into their banking account while I grabbed a pen so I could be ready to write down all the information.

She rattled off a long number.

"American Express." Christine had every detail, down to the four-digit code from the front of the American Express card. "Whoever tried to poison you is pretty stupid to pay with a credit card."

"I don't think they thought they'd get caught. They must've thought my death would be just accepted as death by chocolate." I rolled my eyes. "Thank you for this."

"I'm sorry. I hate to hear all of this." Christine walked me back out to the front of the bakery, where another line had already formed since we'd been in the back. "Let me know what happens. I'll never leave another cake outside to be picked up, that's for sure."

There was no way she was going to let me leave without giving me a bag of her assorted cookies to go.

"I'll keep you posted." I gripped the piece of paper and juggled the cookies and phone. I dialed Hank when I walked outside, stopping at the curb to check out the traffic both ways so I could cross safely to the other side where the library was located. "Hey, it's me." I wedged the phone between my shoulder and ear when I heard his voicemail pick up.

"I wanted to let you know that I got the credit card information from Christine Watson as to who bought the cake. It was ordered and paid for over the internet with specific instructions for it to be left outside to be picked up after hours. There wasn't a name or a real phone number on the order, but the sale went through." I wondered what he was doing that he wasn't able to take my call and sent me to voicemail. "Anyways, call me if you want the number so you can run it."

I slipped the piece of paper in my purse along with the phone and darted across the two lanes. It was a cooler day, and I could feel the temperature had started to slide into those fall-like afternoons.

Abby was the head librarian, but there were a lot of people employed there. I was happy to see she was in the office when I got there and not doing some children's program or one of the tourist events she did once a week to let tourists know the history of the Daniel Boone National Park. They could just go to the national park office to not only get all the history but to also visit the museum.

"To what do I owe this pleasure of my sister-in-law and a treat?" Her eyes focused on the bag.

"I was over at the Cookie Crumble because someone sent me a

poisoned cake." The reaction you'd expect to get from someone after they heard such news was exactly the expression Abby had. "I'm fine, but Shaw Mole isn't. Apparently he came to kill me, by the look of the silencer on his gun, and he had a major sweet tooth. Whoever wanted me dead delivered the cake unseen to my camper."

"So the person who hired Shaw Mole is a different killer?" Abby asked, and she peeked into the bag. "Are these baked without the poison?"

"Yes." I laughed. "Anyways, I went over to see Christine to ask about the cake, but whoever ordered it paid online, left a bogus phone number, and had specific instructions for Christine to leave it outside. Christine knew me, so she thought it was someone who wanted to surprise me, not kill me."

"I can't believe it." Abby yawned before she took a bite of the cookie.

"But now I think that I should talk to you about Bobby Ray." Honestly, Abby looked tired. She was too young to look so worn out, and it wasn't like her to not call me all the time, even after they'd gotten hitched.

Plus, there wasn't much more to ask her about Shaw, and actually it was probably best to give Hank some time to get my voicemail and call me back so I could give him the information.

So slowing down wasn't such a bad idea.

"Oh, Mae." Her hands dropped down into her lap. "I don't know what is wrong with him. He feels some sort of responsibility to her. We had our first fight because I told him that she was the one who left him at the orphanage. Not the other way around. Then she asks for money? What kind of mom is that?" Abby sounded like a bull with the long huffing sounds she was making and the bitter look on her face. "I told him he couldn't use any part of my money to give to her, and I divided up the bills. I told him this is your half, so whatever money you bring in better cover your half of the bills. Then whatever you have left over is yours to do what you want." I didn't like hearing that from her.

"Are you sure that's a good idea?" I questioned. "I mean, I know he makes a decent living, but I'm worried this is going to hurt the two of you."

"No doubt it is." Abby's eyes filled with tears. She pushed the bag of cookies across her desk. "You better take the bag with you, because I'll polish them off in no time. Talk about stress eating. It's all I've done."

"What time do you get off?" I asked.

"I'm off. I don't want to go home and see him working and reworking the bills to give that birth mother of his money." The bitterness poured out of Abby. It was not a normal personality trait of hers either, so it was strange seeing her like this.

"Do you want to come with me?" I lifted my arms in the air. "I'm going to go see Queenie. Dottie said she's in a Jazzercise class, and I'd like to ask her a question about the night of the murder."

"Why not? I even have my tennis shoes under the desk because of the stress eating. I've been walking during my lunch hour." Abby leaned down and picked up the shoes. "I can leave whenever you want. But I'd like to promote Queenie."

I waited for Abby, who was on her phone doing all the hashtag and social media posts in support of Queenie. Abby was a whiz at marketing and was wasting her talents at the library, but she loved books so much she didn't care what kind of money she made.

On our way out the door, I handed the bag of cookies to the employee at the reference desk and told her to enjoy them.

"How are you and Hank?" Abby and I had gotten into the Focus. I drove the car back toward town.

"I think we are good, and he thinks we are good, but there's something weird going on with him that has nothing to do with Judie Doughty." Not that I liked to tell my friends about my love life—I usually didn't share that much—but the situation with Hank seemed to be more than love life.

"Do you want to talk about it?" Abby was always a good listener, but I opted out of telling her anything since I didn't even know what was real myself.

"I'm not even sure. I just feel like something is off." I thought about the voicemail I'd left Ranger Buxley about me doing the article and prayed he didn't call back while I was with Abby or even trying to talk to Queenie.

One thing at a time, I reminded myself now that I'd checked two things off of my very long list.

"Then why don't you tell me why we are going to Jazzercise?" Abby settled back into the seat.

"Queenie said she had seen Angus go into his room right before the fireworks. Did she see Shaw Mole? Glenda Russel had talked to Shaw, so we know he ran off, but did he stop and see Angus? Angus was poisoned. Did the same person who tried to poison me poison Angus? Did we have two killers?"

"Wow. That's a lot of questions. Maybe this whole thing is above the level of the Laundry Club Ladies." Abby had never backed down from a good job of snooping around.

Now I knew she wasn't herself, but how I was going to help her and Bobby Ray stick together? There was no denying there was trouble in paradise.

CHAPTER TWENTY-ONE

Abby and I laughed as soon as we heard the loud and thumping music blaring from the open doors of the undercroft of the Normal Baptist Church.

"I said get your swexy on. That's sweat and sexy. We aren't too old!" Queenie's class today looked like it was seniors. "Take a huge cleansing breath for me today." Queenie squatted as her arms swooped down and around, then her legs straightened when she lifted her arms above her head. "Y'all ready for a parrrr-ty up in here? The Baptists ain't gonna know what hit them, but we do! What is hitting them?"

The older ladies in the class yelled, "Jazzercise babes!"

"Oh my goodness, they've named themselves." Abby giggled a little too loudly, because Queenie looked over at the door and noticed us.

"My oh my, my fit sixty-ish eyes must be in as great shape as my body, because two of my friends are here. I know I'm not seeing things." She continued to swoop and stretch. "Okay, ladies, toes front and tilt your tailbone back as you hold in that belly for good posture."

Queenie did a few ball changes our way, wagged us in, and pointed to a spot in front of her.

"Look down, up. Push that chin down and then up." Queenie talked over the thumping music. "This is your warm-up, ladies. Back to the beginning." Queenie moved elegantly while Abby and I fumbled. "Look at me, ladies! Pull, lift, pull, lift. Now tap the toe."

I wasn't able to look at Abby for fear I'd fall on my face. If this was the warm-up, I hated to see what the next song was going to be.

"Ready? We gonna go." The song transitioned to an even faster beat. "Bounce, ladies! Grab that beat. Bounce."

I tried to imitate Queenie. Her legs were slightly bent as she bounced up and down.

"Got that beat?" she hollered. "Double lunge!" She started bouncing so fast on her toes, lunging forward to the beat a couple of times before switching to the next leg just when I was getting used to the one leg.

"Walk forward with your arms pulling down and pulling out. Now walk backwards doing the same arm movements." Queenie moved so fast, she was back to the forward walk before I'd gotten to the backwards walk. "We are going to do this four times, ladies!"

I couldn't help but look around, and everyone was able to do the moves in step to the music and to Queenie's instruction.

"We gonna march in and out, then I'd like you to sweep that arm up like you're sweeping it up against the wall. Sweep, sweep. March in and out. Now sweep, sweep." Queenie amazed me. "We ain't stopping now, ladies! We are climbing up that ladder! I want you to repeat after me," she instructed them. "I am amazing! I am capable! Exercise is a privilege. Thank your body for moving. Thank your heart for beating!"

I'd have liked to be able to say I was able to keep up with her and the moves, but Jazzercise proved I wasn't in shape nor was I a good dancer. When it came time for the free weight part of the class, I was good at that, but the floor exercises—oh my goodness. I couldn't finish the exercises, so I just lay there begging for the class to be over soon.

"You're going to need a lot more practice, but good for your first time." Queenie wiped her sweaty forehead off with a towel.

"What was with all the motivational mumbo-jumbo you were telling them?" I pointed to her class of seniors, who were all talking amongst themselves.

"They are old like me. We need all the encouragement we can get, but you, you're young and should be able to run circles around us." Queenie grabbed her water bottle and took a long chug from it. "Ahhhh. Feels good, don't it?"

"No. I need some pain reliever." I could already feel my muscles were going to be so achy in the morning. "Look at Abby. She's sitting up against the wall, trying to suck in some air."

"Ah, you two'll be fine. Walk it off." Queenie laughed. "What made you come today of all days?"

"I think whoever killed Angus Coo tried to kill me."

"Shut up." She gasped and grabbed my arm. "What happened?" She took the towel and dabbed at her underarms.

"Let's just say that someone tried to poison me by chocolate." I didn't want to get too much into it here.

"I guess that's a pretty good way to die," she joked. "But it still doesn't answer why you're in my class. You must want something pretty bad to be here after I've begged y'all to come."

"I had nothing better to do, but I'll be sure I do next time." Abby groaned and rubbed her neck.

Queenie and I laughed. I could feel the soreness starting to creep up too.

"You mentioned how you had seen Angus Coo run to his room at the Old Train Station Motel. There was someone who had gone in there later to poison him." I was trying to piece together how it all went but seemed to be missing something.

While Queenie stood there trying to recall, I started to go over everything as I paced in the basement of the undercroft.

"Let's go over this one more time," I told them, and Abby came over. "Judie Doughty had won the lottery but had started to receive death-threatening notes before that. The notes don't even indicate why they are threatening her, which seems odd, but in any case—" I sucked in a deep breath. "Ashley Marzullo, our first victim, actually needed the foal she'd given to the auction to sell for more than what the auctioneer was going to start at, so there was a little tiff between them. But when the shooter aimed at Judie, they accidentally shot Ashley."

"Or did they?" Abby asked. "What if Ashley was also the intended target because whoever hired Shaw Mole also hired him to kill you?"

That made my stomach hurt.

"Keep going." Queenie was doing some sort of stretching move.

"So we have Ashley dead. Then we also have Angus Coo, who was upset because Judie didn't take his highest bid and he needed it for his job, but he was poisoned." I snapped my fingers. "Who would be so jealous of Ashley and Angus Coo to have killed them?"

"You know I did see someone go into Angus's room, but I didn't think anything of it. In fact, I thought maybe Judie had sent them since they'd had that fight." Queenie's face lit up.

"Who was it?" Abby asked.

"It was Evan Doughty." Queenie shocked us all.

CHAPTER TWENTY-TWO

"Evan Doughty?" I asked. "Are you sure?"

"I'm positive." She nodded. "In fact, I think he came into the Caboose Diner and got a couple of glasses of tea or something to go."

"In two glasses?" I asked.

"Yeah. I believe so." She continued to nod. "But you'd have to ask Coke. She didn't have any paper cups. I think she told him to leave the glasses in the room and she'd have house cleaning pick them up in the morning."

"We need to go." I grabbed Abby by the hand.

We hurried out of the undercroft and bolted to the car.

"Do you really think he did it?" Abby asked.

"Of course I do. It does make total sense. He's not going to get the lottery money since it was all poured back into the business, but he is working for the business. Think about it." I couldn't believe how I'd missed the signs. "Ashley said to Judie—I had heard her—she said that if Judie didn't price the foal right, Ashley would make sure that word got around how Judie was a scam artist and the foundation would go under." We jumped into the car, and I pushed my key into the ignition, not even waiting for Abby to completely buckle up before I took off.

"Then when Angus Coo pretty much threatened the same thing after the auction, Evan heard him. He was there for both."

"So you're saying Judie was never the intended target for the events that took place at the event?" Abby was catching on.

"Right. I think whoever is sending Judie these letters isn't even here. It's a separate case. But Evan has been able to use the situation to his advantage and had Ashley and Angus deliberately killed because the two of them were vowing to bring down the company, which would stop his income. He'd have to go back to his old way of life. Judie had told Sally Ann how they were dirt poor before the money had come along, and they had barely been able to get by. But now that they had the foundation and she could help people, it's changed all of their lives by giving them all jobs, and more importantly a purpose in life." I gripped the wheel and headed straight out of town, going toward Fawn Road, which was named after Abby's family and was where the Old Train Station was located. "Can you look at my phone and see if Hank has called me back?"

I hadn't taken my phone into Jazzercise.

I kept my eye on the road, and Abby fiddled with the phone.

"Nothing." She put it back in the cup holder where I'd put it when she and I had left the library before we'd gone to the church. "What are you going to do?"

"About Hank?" I asked.

"Hank? No, about Evan." She wanted to know our strategy once we got to the motel.

"I'm hoping they haven't left, because Agnes told me Al was going to let Judie's entire bunch leave. So I'm hoping they are still there packing up all the stuff. Then I don't know what I'm going to do." I gave her a quick glance before I shifted back to focusing on the road. "Do you have any suggestions?"

"Why don't I go in and ask Coke about the glasses, and maybe you can find Judie's secretary. What's her name?" Abby asked.

"Iona Thatcher," I said.

"Yeah. Her. Maybe you can go see her and ask if she has overheard

Evan throughout this process grumbling or moaning. Men love to have a woman's ear, and if you listen closely to them, they are pretty easy to figure out. Since she knows the inner workings with Judie and never leaves Judie's side, from what you said Delaney Harrison told you, then I bet she's got some opinions." Abby was right. She continued, "By then, hopefully Hank has called you back and he can get out there."

Abby reached down and got her purse off the floorboard. She dug down in it and got her phone. After she looked at it and typed a few things, she put the purse next to her.

"I think you have a great plan." I continued to play the scenario out in my head. I would head out to the barn to see if I saw Evan, then possibly ask Delaney where Judie was, because if I could find Judie after I spotted Evan, I would know where Evan was and could talk to Iona.

Diving deep into my thoughts made the drive go by so fast that before I knew it, we had pulled into the parking lot of the motel. I was happy to see Judie's truck and a few of the horse trailers still in the field, which told me they were still there.

"You go look for Judie, and I'll go to the barn and look for Evan," I told Abby when we got out of the car. She headed toward Judie's room while I darted through the courtyard on my way to the barn.

There was a line of big Ford trucks with horse trailers of varying sizes hooked up to them next to the barn. In the distance, I saw Evan was guiding one of the horses out by the reins, and I walked over to him very cautiously. I knew I had to be very careful as to what I would say.

I patted my back pocket for my phone, just in case I needed it, and realized I'd jumped out of the car and left it in the cup holder. Or at least Abby had put it back in the cup holder.

"Are y'all about to get on your way?" I asked Evan. We were quickly joined by Delaney Harrison, who I needed to get alone so I could ask her a few questions.

"Yep. I guess so. It's been a good fundraiser despite all that's happened." Evan seemed pretty darn pleased with himself. Delaney went back into the barn.

"How so?" I wanted to understand exactly how he thought.

"These horses are so good with veterans, and some local vets had come over to do some therapy. We were able to shoot a couple good commercials. You know"—Evan shook his head—"my mom is a tough cookie. She didn't let all this crime and threats slow down her vision to help people. She could've packed up a couple days ago and thrown up her hands, decided not to continue to use these horses for therapy, cash out and just live, but she didn't do that. I'm pretty proud of her."

"I bet you are." My eyes narrowed.

"It's made me realize that I need to go to school and get a degree in business if I'm going to be part of the organization." Evan had a plan?

His phone rang. He looked at me.

"It's my mom. Said it's urgent. I'll be right back." He headed toward the motel, where I was sure Abby had talked to Judie, leaving me with the chance to go question Delaney about him.

I found her in the barn, cleaning up and putting things in her tack box. She had one that stood upright with the big door and wheels for easy travel.

"Packed up?" I made casual chitchat when I walked through the gated stall door.

"Mm-hmm." She picked up a long tool. "This is a cattle prod."

"Really?" I found it strange she had one. "Do you use those on horses?"

"No. People." She flung it forward and hit me in the side.

An electric shock pulsed through me, knocking the breath out of me. I doubled over. Another poke in the side sent me to the ground, where I lay with my knees up to my chest, heaving for a breath.

"St…" I gasped. My heart raced. "Stop," I moaned almost so low that I wasn't sure if I'd actually said it out loud. "Why?" I found the strength to blurt out one word before she stuck me again in the same spot. I yelled out in pain. My body flung to the side of the barn wall out of reflex from the shock, and I knocked my back into the wall.

"Because you were going to ruin it for me. You and everyone else around here. Don't you understand I love Evan and I won't stop at anything to have him? That means killing you." She lifted her hand in the air to bring the end of the cattle prod back down on me.

"No, you won't!" Abby hollered, swinging an old piece of barnwood and knocking Delaney in the side, forcing her to drop the cattle prod.

I tried to keep my eyes open to see what was going on and prayed Abby was taking down Delaney.

The buzz of the cattle prod going off and the smell of burnt skin curled around me before I heard a thud. I was barely able to open my eyes to see it was Delaney Harrison lying next to me.

"Mae." Abby rushed over to me. "Let me sit you up."

Carefully she helped me get my back up against the wall. I wasn't able to look up at her, but I could hear her heavy breathing as if she were trying to get her wits about her before she slid down the wall next to me.

"I sure didn't see that coming." I held both arms around my waist. My head hung from the pain I was in.

"Before I found you, I talked to Hank," Abby told me. If I could move, I'd have kissed her. "My phone was ringing when I was trying to find you, and when I dug down into my purse, your phone was in there. I must've thought your phone was mine when we were in the car and you had me looking to see if Hank had called. Anyways, Hank was taken aback that I answered, and I told him that you went to find Evan and Delaney because we thought Iona was the killer. We were wrong."

"You think?" I moaned and held my side. "I can't believe how this went down."

"How did you think this was going to happen?" Abby pushed back her long brown hair and slid down the barn wall.

"You know, I guess I made this scenario in my head when we were in the car and really thought it was how it was going to be. I never imagined you would accidentally put my phone in your purse." I leaned over and laid my head on Abby's shoulder. "I'm so glad you're my sister-in-law."

"Abby? Mae?" Hank's frantic voice called out for me.

"We are in the stall!" Abby yelled back, giving way to thudding feet and shuffling hay from the barn's floor.

"Gosh." Hank turned the corner of the stall, pushed the gate all the way open, and ran in to our side. "Are you two hurt?"

"No. We are fine." I managed to give him a weak smile. "Just get her out of here."

Tucker had come in, and Hank pointed to Delaney.

"There she is." Tucker pulled the cuffs from his pants and rushed over to get them on her. She was a bit groggy from the cattle prod but no more hurt than I was.

Al Hemmer and a couple of his deputies followed in behind Tucker and took over, taking Delaney out of the stall.

"How did you figure it out?" I asked.

"Horse tranquilizers in pill form. Then when we saw the footage of a horse trailer and truck going past the Cookie Crumble about the time Christine told us the person who ordered the cake would have picked it up, we knew it was someone from the foundation. So we asked Judie, who drove that truck, and she told us it was Delaney." Tucker had done a great job getting all of it figured out. "Who has horse tranquilizers? Delaney Harrison."

"But why would she do this?" I was at a loss.

"She also wrote the letters, and all of this started much earlier than when Judie won the lottery." Hank took over telling me the story. "The letters Judie had given you were postmarked before the lottery winning, so we started to dig around to that time. That's when we discovered Delaney and Evan were dating. Judie doesn't allow dating within the foundation and pretty much put a stop to it by telling Evan he was going to be cut off and to get a real job."

"Right. And that's when Delaney started to send those threatening letters, only they were just veiled threats so Judie would be scared and rely on Evan being there. Delaney would be by his side, so Judie would accept her." Tucker had nailed down how the actual letters had started.

"That's crazy," I spat.

"Delaney is crazy." Hank nodded. "After Judie won the lottery, she knew Judie wouldn't need Evan to keep seeing her, so she hired Shaw Mole to kill Judie. But she had a change of plans and hired him to kill Ashley Marzullo and Angus Coo because they were going to make problems for the foundation. Because in her mind, Evan was going to take over after Judie was killed, and that was her money ticket. But if Ashley and Angus had made good on their threats, Evan would have had to focus on keeping the foundation afloat, leaving them on the back burner."

"Goodness." I gulped. "The lengths people go to stay in a relationship."

Hank walked over and put his arm around me. "Tell me about it." He hugged me to him.

CHAPTER TWENTY-THREE

"I reckon you made it out alive again." Dottie sat in a chair under the oak tree just outside of the Milkery kitchen. "I never saw the likes of when Hank brought her back to the campground."

Mary Elizabeth and Dottie were talking about yesterday, the whole cattle-prodding incident and my run-in with the real killer, Delaney Harrison.

"I'm just thankful you were there, Dottie." Mary Elizabeth patted my hand. I was sitting next to her on the metal swing.

My stomach and side were still sore. I'd refused to get medical treatment because I knew I was fine and just needed to go home to bed. I had slept all night with Hank and Chester staying over to make sure I didn't need anything if I did wake up.

"She moaned and groaned all night, but Fifi and Chester weren't going to leave her side." Hank stood over me.

"I told her this morning that we could've canceled today now that you're home for good." Mary Elizabeth had gone ahead and hosted the cookout in his honor.

It wasn't going to be too big. Just me, Dottie, Mary Elizabeth, Dawn Gentry, Agnes, and Hank, since Bobby Ray and Abby had decided to stay home because they had a few things to discuss about his birth mother and whatever they'd decided to do about that.

I felt bad for him. No matter what was going on with me, I knew it was going to be a long process dealing with his situation. Abby was pretty shook up yesterday, and she needed some time to be with Bobby Ray.

Even though yesterday was over, Hank and Jerry had met about another case that didn't involve me. Yet.

It seemed like Hank was settled in the new camper, and he still had that darn beard. I'd not had time to ask him about the file and the guy that kept coming around. Honestly, I'd forgotten about it, and it was going to have to wait until I felt better. Nothing seemed urgent.

I was happy that Judie Doughty's case was closed and she was definitely going to press charges outside of the criminal charges that would be brought against Delaney for double murder.

Judie pulled the old I-told-you-so on Evan when Al had put Delaney in the sheriff's car to take her back to the department, where they'd get her transferred to a bigger prison until she awaited trial or just got sentenced. I wasn't sure what Delaney would plead—more than likely she'd go the insanity route, that love had made her do crazy things.

She did spout off how she didn't remember hiring Shaw Mole to kill me, and out of a desperate attempt to make sure I didn't find out about her plan and what she'd done, since I'd been so nosy, she'd laced the cake from the Cookie Crumble with enough horse tranquilizers to kill a sleigh of horses.

Poor Shaw Mole. I figured his weakness to cake and all sweets was justice to all the victims he'd killed in his past as a gun for hire. From what I overheard Tucker and Al saying, there was a lot of paperwork in other cities that had to be dealt with over all the people Shaw had murdered.

Hank had excused himself to go to the bathroom when Agnes Swift had pulled up.

I took the pain and eased up to standing so I could go over and greet her. Plus she'd brought Precious, and I knew Fifi would be so happy.

Fifi and Chester took the slow walk with me to greet her.

"I can't believe you've been keeping my grandson to yourself, but Precious and I couldn't be more thrilled he's back. When I saw him when I got here, I almost didn't recognize him." She tapped her temple. "The old mind plays tricks on this old lady sometimes."

I wanted to tell her that Hank had gone to see her a couple of days ago at the department, or at least that's what he had said. When Agnes told me she'd not seen him, I wondered if she was getting up in age and forgetting a few things, but I didn't want her to overthink her not remembering.

"He is so handsome. Even with the beard." Sadness draped over me at the thought of Agnes getting any form of dementia. It would kill Hank.

"Granny!" Hank waved her over from the kitchen door and checked the grill Mary Elizabeth had put him in charge of before he headed our way.

"It's 'bout time I get to see you," I overheard Agnes say to Hank on her shuffle over. "I can't believe you've been here a few days and didn't come see me."

When I looked at them, Hank put his arm around her, and they embraced. I could see his lips moving underneath all of his fur, and the happiness on her face lifted my heart.

My stomach growled, and my phone rang at the same time. I looked at my phone and saw it was the ranger from Mammoth Cave returning my call.

I hesitated and thought I should just let Hank handle whatever they needed from them. But just as always, my curious side got the better of me.

"Hello?" I answered.

"This is Ranger Buxley from the Mammoth Cave district, returning your call," he said.

"Yes. Hold on just a second. I need to get to a quiet place." I walked to the side of the bed-and-breakfast, away from the group. The pain shot through my side and down my legs, but I made it to a quiet spot.

"I'm sorry, yes. I'm doing an article on the man that went missing." I continued to use the same cover-up lie I'd used when I had called him to get some information.

"The best thing media can do for us right now is get us any information on Ranger Hank Sharp. He was the lead in the investigation. He's gone missing, and we haven't been able to track him down. He's got a few leads we need, so the more we get his face out there, the better."

"Is Ranger Sharp a suspect?" The pain in my heart overrode the pain from the cattle prods.

"He's definitely an interest that we need to clear. We've connected a few things to him and need to talk to him, which is why we are asking the public to help us. Anything your publication can do will be of help. Ranger Sharp is a smart man. He can live out in the woods for a very long time on his resourcefulness." I couldn't believe what he was telling me.

"And when did you notice Ranger Sharp left?" I refused to believe what I was hearing.

"Just a couple of days ago. We've been scouring the Mammoth Cave area. We found his camper, but it appears he's plucked it clean, cleared everything out, which is why we are now expanding our search throughout Kentucky."

"Okay. Let me get with my editor, and maybe I can get down there to do the story." I kept up the lie even though now I had my answers. What could I do? Tell him Hank Sharp was in the room next to where I was?

The beard, the mustache, the new camper. All the things that didn't make sense started to add up. He took a job from Jerry that paid under the table.

And the man that came to the campground, asking me all sorts of questions. I gulped and glanced over at Hank and Agnes.

My thoughts curled back to when he said he'd gone to the sheriff's department to see if they'd gotten any video from the guests at the fundraiser. He'd said Agnes hadn't seen anything, so he was going to ask Al. Did he lie to me and Jerry?

"Mae, honey." Hank walked around the corner of the bed-and-breakfast.

I looked at him. My hands fell to my sides.

"What's wrong? Who was that on the phone?"

"Did you know you're wanted for the disappearance of a man by the name of Walter Adams in Mammoth Cave?"

His jaw dropped.

"Yes," he whispered, not looking at me.

Talk about trust.

THE END

If you enjoyed reading this book as much as I enjoyed writing it then be sure to return to the Amazon page and leave a review.

Go to Tonyakappes.com for a full reading order of my novels and while there join my newsletter. You can also find links to Facebook, Instagram and Goodreads.

I'd love to continue your stay in Happy Trails Campground. You never know what kinda trouble Mae is gonna get into next!

Keep scrolling to read a sneak peek of Jackets, Jack-O-Lantern, and Justice or get your copy today on Amazon or read for FREE in Kindle Unlimited.

Chapter One of Book Twenty Two
Jackets, Jack-O-Lantern, & Justice

"A man is dead. Ranger John Buxley has been snooping around. You have a beard. You have a new camper." I paced back and forth underneath the full moon on the edge of the lake in Happy Trails Campground.

If my adrenaline hadn't been kicked in high gear, the rustling leaves and crunch of layers of pine needles that'd started to fall with the crisp cool fall air, not to mention twigs underfoot of something in the deep forest, I'd gotten myself inside of the camper.

But no. I'd just found out Hank Sharp, my boyfriend, was wanted for questioning in a murder case a few hundred miles from the Daniel Boone National Forest where I owned and ran Happy Trails Campground in Normal, Kentucky.

"Yes. I did get rid of my camper because I needed to not be found. Yes. I've grown a beard so no one from the Mammoth Cave District would recognize me."

I had no idea where this was going because he'd all but said he killed the guy while he was a ranger in that area.

"And I haven't gone to the sheriff's department to see Granny because I didn't know if John Buxley had gotten to Al Hemmer yet." Hank sat on the rock around the large campfire I had next to the lake for the guests to enjoy, but truth be told, I was a smidgen upset with him, so I suggested we sit outside instead of one of our campers so I could keep the distance between us.

My eyes slide back to the crackling fire behind him. He was saying all sorts of excuses and I'd like to say I heard him, but all I could think of was giving him a great big shove back into the red, yellow, and orange flames.

"Mae," he said my name and looked back at the fire to see where my eyes had strayed. "I think I'll move."

"Good idea." I started to pace again. "Do you know what kind of position you've put my business in? Forget me. What about the camp-ground? I have all of these tourists staying here and it wouldn't look so great if it was raided and dragging someone out in cuffs." I threw my hands up in the air, then planted them on my waist as I looked at him, where he was now sitting in one of the many Adirondack chairs along the banks. "I have employees to think of and my home is here. If I harbor a criminal, a killer," my voice rose and octave, "they will put me in jail and my campground." I pointed a finger at him and gave him a good scolding. "I've worked hard for this place. Or do I have to remind you?"

"Oh no." He shook his head. "I was the first person who met you here, remember?"

How could I forget? At that time and many jobs past, Hank was an agent and my ex-now dead-Ponzi scheming husband had escaped from prison, only to be found dead, floating in the very lake where Hank and I were at this moment.

"And exactly this. You thought I was harboring Paul," I reminded him how he accused me of hiding the ex. "And now Ranger Buxley thinks I'm hiding you."

"That's what I'm trying to say. You aren't hiding me." He ran his hands over his thick black hair. The moonlight catch his strong jawline just right, his green eyes sparkled.

I swallowed hard trying not to give into his good looks and let him off the hook. There had to be a reasonable explanation as to why Ranger Buxley wanted to find Hank, and an equally reasonable expla-nation as to why Hank hasn't let Ranger Buxley find him.

Which brought me back to thinking Hank has killed the man in question.

"Go on." I stopped packing and stood in front of him with my arms crossed, tapping my right foot to exaggerate just how aggravated I'd become.

"They aren't looking for me." Hank eased back into the chair. He placed his palms down on the wide wooden arms. His chest lifted as he took in a breath.

"They are looking for me." The woman's voice was almost a whisper behind us. Like the whisper had caught on the chilly breeze as it fluttered past my ears and trickled across the lake.

The shadowy figure was about to come into the moon's light and when it did, I couldn't've been more shocked.

"Ellis Sharp?" I questioned when Hank's sister came into view.

Grab your copy of Jackets, Jack-O-Lantern, & Justice today on Amazon or read from free with Kindle Unlimited.

RECIPES AND CAMPING HACKS FROM MAE WEST AND THE LAUNDRY CLUB LADIES AT THE HAPPY TRAILS CAMPGROUND IN NORMAL KENTUCKY.

Southern Olive Nut Spread

Ingredients

- Cream cheese
- Mayonnaise
- Green olives with pimentos
- Juice from olives
- Chopped pecans
- Pepper

Directions

1. In a mixing bowl, combine all ingredients. If your cream cheese is soft enough, you will not need a mixer. I had no problem mixing this with a spoon.
2. Chill in refrigerator for 2 hours.
3. Serve with wheat thins, Hawaiian rolls, Ritz crackers, or bread for small sandwiches.

Camping Hack #1

Happy Trails Campground offers all amenities to its guests. It's rare to have everything in one campground, and when they do, it can be costly. Not all towns have a Laundry Club or Laundry Club Ladies. In this case, what do you do? How do you wash your clothes?

Easy!

Take a five-gallon bucket with a lid. Cut a small square in the middle of the lid. Get a toilet plunger and put it in the bucket with the handle sticking out of the closed lid.

When you need to wash an item of clothing, open the lid and take out the plunger. Put the piece of clothing in, add detergent, and add enough water to cover the item of clothing. Put the plunger in the bucket, put the lid on, and move the plunger around in the bucket.

Take the piece of clothing out and hang it to dry!

Salsa and Corn Dumpling Soup

Ingredients

- 1/2 cup tomato powder
- 2 tablespoons dried onion flakes
- 1/4 teaspoon garlic powder
- 1 to 3 teaspoons dried cilantro
- 1 teaspoon dried oregano
- 1 1/2 teaspoons cumin, divided
- 1/2 teaspoon red chili flakes
- 1 bell pepper, diced and dehydrated (optional)
- 1 cup blended tomatoes, cilantro, jalapeños, dehydrated (optional)
- 1/2 cup cornmeal
- 1/2 cup flour
- 1/4 cup milk powder
- 2 teaspoons baking powder
- 2 tablespoons Parmesan cheese, grated

Directions

1. Pour 4 cups of water into pot and bring to boil. Add soup ingredients to the water and lower heat to a simmer.
2. Add 1/2 cup of water to dumpling Ziplock bag and seal. Knead the contents of the bag until dough is evenly mixed. It will be a thick, sticky batter.
3. Spoon batter directly on top of the simmering broth and cover for 10 minutes. Don't peek!
4. The dumplings are ready when they are puffed up and cooked through the middle. Cook for 5 additional minutes if the middle still seems doughy.

Camping Hack #2

Sometimes there's just not enough space to bring bottles of items from home. Shampoos and toothpastes come in travel size, but soap and shower gels are hard to find. A perfect camping hack is to get a sponge, syringe, and shower gel. Fill the syringe with your shower gel and inject it several times into the sponge. Put the sponge in a Ziploc bag. Get the sponge out during each shower, and you've got instant gel.

Dutch Oven Stuffed Peppers

Ingredients

- 6 bell peppers
- 2 tablespoons olive oil, plus more for greasing the Dutch oven
- 1 large onion, chopped
- 2 cloves garlic, minced
- 10 ounces mushrooms, chopped
- 14 ounces vegetarian ground meat (or real meat, if you like)
- 4 cups cooked rice
- 1 15-ounce can tomato sauce
- salt and pepper, to taste
- 2 tablespoons ketchup
- 3/4 cup shredded extra-sharp cheddar

Directions

1. Grease your Dutch oven. Get your campfire going and prep it so there is eventually a nice bed of hot coals to place your Dutch oven on.
2. Cut the tops off of the peppers. Remove the seeds from the main part of the pepper and set them aside. Trim the remaining pepper off of the pepper tops. Chop and reserve for stuffing.
3. Sauté the onion in olive oil until translucent. Add garlic, mushrooms, and chopped peppers. Cook until vegetables are softened, about 5 minutes. Stir in the veggie meat and cook for a few minutes more. Mix in the rice and about half the can of tomato sauce. Season with salt and pepper.
4. Place the stuffing inside of the peppers and then into the Dutch oven. If you have any additional stuffing, you can put it

around the peppers (just make sure you greased your Dutch oven well).

5. Add the ketchup to the remaining tomato sauce and stir to combine. Spoon some of the tomato sauce mixture on top of the stuffed peppers. Sprinkle the peppers with cheese.

6. Place Dutch oven on the hot coals, making sure it is stable and level. You may have to shift some of the coals around, or add a rock under the Dutch oven to get it just right. Cook the peppers until they're softened and the stuffing is heated through.

Camper/ Camping Hack #3

We all have cell phones now. When we hike during our camping trips, we sometimes come across water that we weren't expecting. Oh no! Your phone fell into the water. No rice? No problem!

Why? Because all of those little silicon packets that come in your shoes or pretty much anything you buy—well, save those! You can put a phone in a baggie full of those silicon packs, and guess what? It works better than a bag full of rice!

Lanterns, Lakes & Larceny
Book Club Questions

Question 1:

Hank Sharp has come back into Mae's life. He parked his camper, his NEW camper in his old space before he even called Mae. Now what?

Thoughts? I felt he was being a little too confident in his assumption!

Question 2:

Although Hank was only gone a few months, Mae wasn't expecting his change in appearance. This was an interesting develop and left Mae with some unasked questions.

If you were Mae, would you have doubts or just be glad Hank was back in her life??

Question 3:

Bobby Ray and Abby are experiencing some growing pains in their marriage now that Bobby Ray's birth mother in his life and constantly asking for money.

Mae wasn't sure what to say to either of them. Would you have given them any advice or would you just listen and acknowledge?

Question 4:

According to Hank, he has returned to Normal, not only because he missed Mae, but to help Jerry Truman, in his new PI Business. Apparently, Jerry has a high-profile case involving a wealthy client who has been receiving death threats. They have decided to hire Mae as a consultant on the case.

How did you feel about this change in hiring Mae? In the past Hank, would not be on board with Mae assisting.

Question 5:

While working the fundraiser, Help for Horses, that Jerry's client, Judie Doughty had established, tempers where flaring. When an attempt was made on Judie's life, it wasn't Judie who was shot but an attendee.

This surprised me since Judie was the one receiving the death threats. Was the bullet really for her and the shooter missed?

Question 6:

While at the fundraiser, Mae and Hank are discussing The Chicken Fest. A little trivia about The Chicken Fest! "The entire state of Kentucky celebrated Chicken Fest, which was homage to Colonel Sanders, and his famous fried chicken he brought to our great state." I haven't lived in Kentucky for very long, and I had no idea there was a festival to honor Colonel Sanders! In case you would like to attend, the festival is on September 23rd in London, Kentucky.

Does your state have a special festival in honor of something or someone?

Question 7:

With the fundraiser having one victim, another follows. Now there are two to murders investigate. It turns out the killer, Shaw Mole, was on the FBI's Most Wanted list. Shaw ends up dead eating a chocolate cake in Mae's office while waiting for her.

The cake made for Mae and paid for by an anonymous person. Mae knew that Christine from the Cookie Crumble didn't poison her, what were your thoughts as to who poisoned the cake?

Question 8:

Mae discovers there is a Ranger from the Mammoth Cave district where Hank worked asking questions around Normal regarding Hank's whereabouts. He let Mae know Hank is a person of interest, in the murder of Walter Adams, the same name on some of the files Mae found in Hank's camper.

Mae begins to question Hank's reason for showing back up in Normal. What were your thoughts, suspicions?

Question 9:

My favorite parts of the book are always the "Dottie-isms,"

This time when Dottie was speaking about Hank she said: "That boy's got more moves than a slinky going down an escalator." I found several in this book that I enjoyed.

Did you have one this time?

Question 10:

Without telling us who the killer was, did you figure this one out, or was it a complete surprise? Pretty much a surprise to me. I thought I knew, then confirmed at the end.

Yes or No

A NOTE FROM TONYA

Thank y'all so much for this amazing journey we've been on with all the fun cozy mystery adventures! We've had so much fun and I can't wait to bring you a lot more of them. When I set out to write about them, I pulled from my experiences from camping, having a camper, and fond memories of camping.

Readers ask me if there's a real place like those in my books. Sadly, no. It's a combination of places I've stayed and would own if I could.

XOXO ~ Tonya

For a full reading order of Tonya Kappes's Novels, visit
Tonyakappes.com

BOOKS BY TONYA
SOUTHERN HOSPITALITY WITH A SMIDGEN OF HOMICIDE

Camper & Criminals Cozy Mystery Series

All is good in the camper-hood until a dead body shows up in the woods.

BEACHES, BUNGALOWS, AND BURGLARIES
DESERTS, DRIVING, & DERELICTS
FORESTS, FISHING, & FORGERY
CHRISTMAS, CRIMINALS, AND CAMPERS
MOTORHOMES, MAPS, & MURDER
CANYONS, CARAVANS, & CADAVERS
HITCHES, HIDEOUTS, & HOMICIDES
ASSAILANTS, ASPHALT & ALIBIS
VALLEYS, VEHICLES & VICTIMS
SUNSETS, SABBATICAL AND SCANDAL
TENTS, TRAILS AND TURMOIL
KICKBACKS, KAYAKS, AND KIDNAPPING
GEAR, GRILLS & GUNS
EGGNOG, EXTORTION, AND EVERGREEN
ROPES, RIDDLES, & ROBBERIES
PADDLERS, PROMISES & POISON
INSECTS, IVY, & INVESTIGATIONS
OUTDOORS, OARS, & OATH
WILDLIFE, WARRANTS, & WEAPONS
BLOSSOMS, BBQ, & BLACKMAIL
LANTERNS, LAKES, & LARCENY
JACKETS, JACK-O-LANTERN, & JUSTICE
SANTA, SUNRISES, & SUSPICIONS
VISTAS, VICES, & VALENTINES
ADVENTURE, ABDUCTION, & ARREST
RANGERS, RVS, & REVENGE

A CHARMING SPELL
A CHARMING MAGIC
A CHARMING SECRET
A CHARMING CHRISTMAS (novella)
A CHARMING FATALITY
A CHARMING DEATH (novella)
A CHARMING GHOST
A CHARMING HEX
A CHARMING VOODOO
A CHARMING CORPSE
A CHARMING MISFORTUNE
A CHARMING BLEND (CROSSOVER WITH A KILLER COFFEE COZY)
A CHARMING DECEPTION

Mail Carrier Cozy Mystery Series

Welcome to Sugar Creek Gap where more than the mail is being delivered.

STAMPED OUT
ADDRESS FOR MURDER
ALL SHE WROTE
RETURN TO SENDER
FIRST CLASS KILLER
POST MORTEM
DEADLY DELIVERY
RED LETTER SLAY

About Tonya

Tonya has written over 100 novels, all of which have graced numerous bestseller lists, including the USA Today. *Best known for stories charged with emotion and humor and filled with flawed characters, her novels have garnered reader praise and glowing critical reviews. She lives with her husband and a very spoiled rescue cat named Ro. Tonya grew up in the small southern Kentucky town of Nicholasville. Now that her four boys are grown men, Tonya writes full-time in her camper she calls her SHAMPER (she-camper).*

Learn more about her be sure to check out her website tonyakappes.com. Find her on Facebook, Twitter, BookBub, and Instagram

Sign up to receive her newsletter, where you'll get free books, exclusive bonus content, and news of her releases and sales.

If you liked this book, please take a few minutes to leave a review now! Authors (Tonya included) really appreciate this, and it helps draw more readers to books they might like. Thanks!

Made in United States
Troutdale, OR
12/26/2023

16413202R00090